"Any clue yet about who it could be?"

"Not yet," Michael said. "Looks like the body was buried years ago. The spring runoff was especially high this year, which is probably why Maisie found the remains." He glanced down at the damp, newly bathed dog at his feet. "If not for her, they might never have been found."

Janna looked at her daughter and lowered her voice. "Did you find any signs of the man I saw on our property?"

Michael shook his head. "We've been scouring the area, but no luck so far. The rain probably helped cover his tracks. You couldn't see any identifying features?"

"Not even what he was wearing, really—with the rain and the distance, it just looked like he was wearing a dark, hooded jacket of some kind." Janna pensively worried at her lower lip. "And I didn't see him near the burial site. Maybe he was just passing through."

"Possibly," Michael said.

"And he might not even be the same guy I saw the night before. A coincidence, nothing more."

But a coincidence didn't seem likely. And given the look in Michael's eyes, he felt the same way.

ROXANNE RUSTAND,

an award-winning author of fifteen books, feels delighted and honored at the opportunity to write for Steeple Hill's Love Inspired Suspense line.

Her first manuscript won a Romance Writers of America Golden Heart Award for Best Long Contemporary. Her second was a Golden Heart finalist and was published in 1999. She has presented writing workshops at writers' conferences from coast to coast and is a member of the American Christian Fiction Writers Association, the Faith, Hope and Love Chapter of RWA, Authors Guild, and Novelists Inc.

Roxanne has a master's degree in nutrition and works as a registered dietitian for a residential psychiatric facility. She and her husband have three children and a multitude of dogs, cats and horses. They live on an acreage in the Midwest, where there's never a dull moment. When there's a quiet one, you can usually find her with her nose in a book. She can be reached through her Web site at www.roxannerustand.com.

ROXANNE RUSTAND

Hard Evidence

Steeple
Hill®

Published by Steeple Hill Books™

STEEPLE HILL BOOKS

Steeple
Hill®

ISBN-13: 978-0-373-44271-3
ISBN-10:   0-373-44271-8

HARD EVIDENCE

www.SteepleHill.com

Printed in U.S.A.

Peace I leave with you; my peace I give to you. I do not give to you as the world gives. Do not let your hearts be troubled and do not be afraid.
—*John* 14:27

With heartfelt thanks to Lyn Cote, a patient and
generous mentor, wonderful writer
and a dear friend.
And with deepest thanks to my family—
Larry, Andy, Brian and Emily, who understood
how much this dream meant to me and have been
encouraging and supportive every step of the way.
Blessings to you all!

ONE

Janna McAllister swept a cobweb away from her ear, blew at the damp tendrils of hair trailing over her forehead and stared at the three mice sitting on the kitchen counter of Cabin Ten.

They stared right back, whiskers twitching, paws folded in front of their little chests, probably even more surprised than she was. But it wasn't the mice that worried her.

She gazed past them to the candy wrappers and soda cans on the counter.

Snow Canyon Lodge had been closed for a good fifteen years, though the cabins had been empty for longer than that. There shouldn't have been any sign of recent human habitation.

And yet…the padlock on the door had been pried off and someone had been in here recently, given the brand names on those wrappers. Hikers? High school kids out for a lark?

Considering what she'd found in a cupboard, she tried not to dwell on other, darker possibilities.

But the people who'd broken in were long gone. She had a job to do, and not much time to get it done. She couldn't afford to let *anyone* stand in her way.

Determination had taken on a whole new meaning, now that she was a single mom, dealing with an ex-husband who could afford little financial support, plus the care of her elderly mother.

Setting her jaw, she continued her inspection of the property with a clipboard in hand, working backward from the most distant cabins toward the ones near the lodge.

Cabins Four and Five had miraculously withstood years of Wyoming's snow and wind and sun, but precious few of the others would be usable without a lot of work…and then only after she hauled away truckloads of trash and moldering furniture. Two of the cabins were just shy of needing demolition.

The main lodge would take months of cleaning, repairs and redecorating to fully restore.

She'd clearly been naive, thinking she could leave her career in Minneapolis the day after Rylie finished school and be ready for business in a few weeks.

Lord, I feel you led me here—and that this place is your answer to my prayers for a new life for Rylie and me. Please help me handle all of this, because I'm sure going to need Your help.

"Mom! Someone's here! *Hurry!*" Rylie's breath-less, excited words floated through the torn screen door of Cabin Three. "I think it's important!"

The nine-year-old's high-pitched voice sent the mice scampering across the buckled vinyl countertops and over the far edge like lemmings over a cliff.

"Just a minute," Janna called out. The last thing the child needed to see was mice. She was already terrified of spiders and ladybugs, thanks to an older boy who'd teased her with both on the school bus.

Janna gingerly stepped around piles of old news-papers, tractor parts and a peach crate filled with grimy Mason canning jars to peer into the back room of the cabin.

She sneezed once—twice—three times at the eddies of dust stirred up by her shoes.

A sagging iron bed filled most of the space. Its stained mattress undoubtedly provided lodging for immeasurable varieties of vermin—and possibly *dozens* of little relatives of the three mice she'd just met. There was no way she wanted to set foot in that room.

Faced with the hard reality of her new life in this remote corner of her mother's ranch, she was torn be-tween tears and incredulous laughter.

"Mom!" Rylie's voice was closer now. A mo-ment later footsteps raced across the lopsided porch of the cabin, and the door squealed open. Rylie stood in the doorway as Maggie, her little white

highland terrier-beagle mix, barreled inside. "You should *see*."

Expecting a feed delivery or possibly something from FedEx, Janna managed a weary smile. Rylie was done with school for the summer and there were no neighborhood kids in the area, so even deliveries were exciting when no one else was around. "Must be about as good as a birthday present, whatever it is."

"It's a man who looks like he could be in a *movie*. And he's got another guy with him, too."

"Really." Janna dusted off her hands and lifted Rylie's chin to study the smudges across her cheeks and brow. Like all the McAllister women, Rylie had the family's green eyes, strawberry-blond hair and petite, delicate build, but she was defiantly in her tomboy phase. "Where have you been?"

"The barn. Up in the loft."

At least there, the rodents were kept at bay by an extended family of cats…and Rylie hadn't seen any spiders.

Janna stifled another sneeze. "Why don't you run up to the lodge and check on your grandma Claire. And I'll—" Janna started out the door, but faltered to a stop when she caught sight of the gleaming black Ford 250 club cab parked over by the lodge.

A tall, dark-haired man leaned against its front fender, his booted feet crossed at the ankles, one elbow propped on the hood. His Stetson tipped low over his forehead, and sunglasses shaded his eyes, but even from where Janna was standing, she could see that the strong jaw and sharp angle of his cheek-bones promised that this was one good-looking guy.

Probably a very *lost* good-looking guy, given the out-of-state plates on his truck. Though per-haps he was one of the rich Californians who'd been flooding the area over the past decade, buying up family owned ranches and driving up land values with their palatial homes. According to Janna's sisters, their mother had been pressured to sell out by several of them already—investors who'd apparently thought an elderly woman would be easy prey.

They'd all met their match in Claire McAllister. And if this guy had similar intentions, he'd find the same was true of her daughter.

Janna strolled across the wiry, sunburned grass to the gravel road that ran past the cabins down to the main ranch road, with Maggie trotting at her side. "Can I help you?"

He'd been staring at the massive, jagged peaks of the Rockies to the west. Farther north, the Teton Range rose dramatically from a level valley floor, but here there were pine-covered foothills with ranches tucked into hidden valleys. He flashed a smile at her. "This is Snow Canyon Resort, right?"

Resort sounded pretentious, given the state of things, but through the smoked glass of the truck's backseat she could see the outlines of luggage and a suit bag hanging behind the driver's seat. An uneasy premonition swept through her. "R-i-i-ight."

"Great." He pushed away from the truck, slipped off his sunglasses and strolled over to offer a handshake. "Michael Robertson."

At closer range she could see his hair was black, his eyes the color of aged brandy flecked with gold. But while some good-looking men seemed to bask in self-satisfaction, this one radiated a level of warmth and openness that surprised her.

She dusted her hand against her faded jeans and shook his hand, trying not to be mesmerized by that low, rich voice or the deep, slashing dimples that bracketed his mouth when he smiled. "Janna McAllister."

He studied her expectantly for a moment. "My son Ian and I have reservations," he said at last. "I called three weeks ago."

Three weeks ago? She and Rylie hadn't even arrived in Wyoming then, so he must have called the ranch office down at the home place, where her sister Tessa still lived.

"You probably talked to Claire—my mother." She darted a look toward the rambling log-and-fieldstone lodge. "I think there's been a mistake."

"I asked for a confirmation number, but the woman I talked to said it wasn't necessary."

Claire certainly hadn't written anything down. The

pristine reservation book was still in its cellophane wrapper, ready for the day when the rustic resort could be fully reopened, but that was a long time away. And so far, Janna had managed to restore just a few rooms in the lodge. "I'm sorry, but—"

The man frowned as he lifted a folded sheet of paper from the back pocket of his jeans and shook it open with one hand before holding it out. "I asked her to fax me some sort of confirmation, anyway, just to be sure."

Janna accepted the paper. Sure enough, it was Snow Canyon Ranch letterhead, with Claire's familiar looping scrawl. And it said…

"Oh, dear," Janna muttered under her breath.

The man glanced impatiently at his watch. "I've essentially got a contract here, signed by the owner of the ranch. A two-bedroom cabin for three full months—from June first through September first."

And according to her mother's almost indecipherable script, she'd agreed to a five-hundred-dollar penalty if either party broke the contract early.

Janna closed her eyes briefly, mentally cataloging the state of the ten cabins trailing up into the foothills, and wished she hadn't started playing with the design of a promotional Web site before she left Minneapolis. "You found us online?"

"Exactly." His friendly tone took on the edge of a man accustomed to taking command. A man who obviously needed a long-term place to stay, and who'd consider this makeshift contract and preposterous penalty an ironclad agreement. "So, is there a problem? I hope not—there's not another place like this within thirty miles of town."

"No…" She took a steadying breath. "I just wasn't aware of the reservation, and the cabins aren't quite ready for guests. But we'll soon be reopening the main lodge as a B&B. You'd be welcome there for a day or so until I can have your cabin ready."

His gaze flickered toward the barn and corral, where a tall, lanky teenager was hanging over the fence to look at a horse. "You have an extra room for my son, as well?"

"Absolutely, and your meals will be on me until we can get you settled properly. We've got a nice guest dining room where we can serve you."

She bit her lower lip as she visualized all of the moving boxes still stacked in that room, and hoped he'd want to dine fashionably late tonight. *Very* late. "I know it's an inconvenience, having to settle in twice, but I'd be happy to help with that."

"No problem." He called to his son, then turned to open the back door of his truck. Draping a suit bag over the top of the open door, he pulled out several suitcases and two duffel bags. "I'm just glad this is going to work out."

"It will. My family and I live in the north wing, and you'll be on the second floor, center. You'll have plenty of peace and quiet during your vacation," Janna assured him as she hefted the weight of the smallest duffel and swung it over her shoulder.

"Actually, I start work as interim sheriff on Monday, while Sheriff Brownley is away on long-term disability leave. The office is in Wolf Creek."

Janna whistled. "That's quite a commute."

"I bought a house on the edge of town, but it needs a lot of work before we can move in." His son ambled up to the truck, clearly trying to mask a definite limp, and grabbed two suitcases. "Ian, this is Janna McAllister, our innkeeper."

She offered him a warm smile. "Hi, Ian."

The boy barely nodded, his head downcast.

"I see you like horses."

He lifted a shoulder in silent response.

He appeared to be about sixteen or seventeen, with his dad's dark hair and eyes. She glimpsed heavy scarring down one side of his face and beneath the cuff of his long-sleeved T-shirt before he ducked his head and turned away, clearly self-conscious.

Michael rested a hand on the boy's shoulder. "Ian is looking forward to some trail riding during his summer vacation. Do we talk to you about that?"

"That's my middle sister, Tessa. She's gone for weeks at a time, leading pack trips up into the high country, but she'll be back at her place on Saturday."

Ian gave his dad a bored look, his mouth curled in derision.

Michael frowned, obviously reminding him to watch his manners. "I'm sure that will be fine. Thanks."

Janna guessed the boy hadn't been entirely cooperative about moving to Wyoming. "In the meantime I could saddle up Frosty for you, if you'll promise to stay up around the corrals. She's in her twenties and safe for anyone."

Ian dug the toe of his Nike into a tuft of wiry grass. "I know how to ride," he mumbled. "I'm not gonna fall off or anything."

"You look like an athletic kid," she assured him. "It's just that people get lost all too easily if they stray off the trails around here. Come on up to the lodge, and I'll show you your rooms."

Janna turned for the lodge and pretended she didn't hear the brief, sharp exchange between father and son. Ahead, she could see her mother standing at her bedroom window with a stern expression.

Though Claire had grudgingly agreed to Janna's long-term lease of the abandoned resort, she'd scoffed at the idea that it could be built into a viable business once again. She'd also been highly resentful of her three daughters' insistence that she needed supervision—but that was no surprise. Even from their early childhoods, she'd been cool and distant, always insisting that they use her first name. Refusing to brook any interference.

The unexpected arrival of these guests was just one more example of her advancing forgetfulness. Forgotten phone calls, lost credit card statements, missing car keys—the situation was getting precarious.

And now strangers moving into the lodge—however brief their stay—might either trigger Claire's ingrained western hospitality, or escalate her paranoia and confusion.

Janna said a silent prayer as she opened the front door of the lodge. "Hey, mother," she announced loudly enough for Claire to hear. "We've got company!"

The rustic lodge had once boasted twenty rooms for guests, but now the south wing was unusable due to heavy water damage from the neglected leaks in the roof. Janna had settled Claire, Rylie and herself in the north wing, away from the public areas of the lodge.

The rooms in the center of the building, which opened onto a balcony overlooking the spacious lobby area and fireplace below, were the only ones ready for guests.

She waved a hand toward the massive, two-story stone fireplace, the spacious social area of the lobby and French doors leading into a small, public dining area. "You and your son are welcome to make yourselves at home. The furniture is a tad sparse right now, but I hope to be making changes very soon."

Michael surveyed the exposed log beams, burnished gold with age, and the sun filtering in through the dozens of high windows. "Beautiful workmanship," he said. "Looks good and solid."

"It was my grandfather's dream for his old age—a nice, quiet little business for him to run. He chose the most distant, scenic spot on his ranch—miles from the main house and barns—and found good managers to run it. It was once a popular destination, I guess."

"What happened?"

"He died at sixty, and my mom's inheritance included the resort, the home where we all grew up and a thousand acres. She was swamped just running her ranch and raising us girls, though, and some of the lodge managers she hired weren't all that great. The place eventually went into a downhill spiral, then finally closed."

He shook his head. "That's a shame."

"Yeah, I know. But my sisters and I were too young to take it over, and all of us had different dreams back then, anyway. Now Leigh is in vet school, Tessa runs the ranch and an outfitting company, and I've taken over this place."

"You have you work cut out for you." Studying the mountains through the windows, he smiled. "The view is incredible though. You'll be overrun with guests."

"I hope so," she said fervently. She grabbed some keys from the front desk and started up the open staircase to the second floor.

She showed Ian into a pine-paneled room with blue gingham curtains and a red, white and blue quilt. "Will this be okay?"

He took one look, then glared over his shoulder at his father and dropped his duffel to the floor with a thud. "There isn't even a TV," he muttered. "What about my PlayStation? I'm gonna be stuck here all summer and—"

"Ian." Michael frowned at him. Then he directed an apologetic smile at Janna. "It's been a long trip, I'm afraid. I figured there wouldn't be a TV in our cabin, but I brought a small one so he could play his video games on it. Can I bring it in for him?"

The tension between father and son was palpable, and Janna found herself wondering about the absent Mrs. Robertson. Perhaps there had been a difficult divorce like her own, and this was an infrequent father-son summer. The two sure didn't seem to have much rapport.

"No problem, of course. We don't have good reception for television stations, but the games should be fine. We also have lots of movies on DVD."

The boy shrugged and shut the door behind him.

Embarrassed for his father, Janna quickly moved on to the next room and opened the door, then held out the key. "These rooms each have a private bath, and the linens are already stocked. If there's anything else you need, just holler."

He accepted the key with a nod of thanks. "We'll be fine."

Memories flooded back as she descended the stairs. She'd visited here as a child, when it was a bustling, popular place for families. At the time, it had been managed by the Websters, a congenial older couple, who had always welcomed her with open arms, along with warm cookies and milk.

Those cozy images had sustained her through the recent trials of rapidly packing up the remnants of her married life in Minneapolis and the long, cross-country trip, but the future didn't seem so rosy now.

Her cursory tour of the place over spring break hadn't quite prepared her for the truly daunting tasks ahead…or for the fact that someone had been in these buildings not long ago…*without* permission.

She shivered, recalling the lurid magazines and stash of empty vodka bottles that she'd discovered in Cabin Ten. The empty shotgun casings, and a splattering of faded stains on the floor.

Something had been going on here.

Probably just a group of hunters who'd partied through a drunken weekend, she told herself firmly trying to stop her imagination from running wild with other possibilities.

Whoever those intruders were, they hadn't been here long ago.

And she would be praying that they never, ever come back.

TWO

"You're sure you'll be okay here today?" Michael studied his son over a table laden with fresh fruit, plates of cheddar cheese and ham omelets, and a basket of fragrant, homemade cinnamon rolls. "I can stay home today, if you want. We could go hiking."

Ian shrugged and continued cutting his food into ever smaller bits. As far as Michael could tell, the boy hadn't actually eaten a single bite, but at least he'd agreed to come downstairs to the dining room of the lodge.

"Or we could go buy our fishing licenses and start looking for some good trout streams."

"I'm seventeen, Dad. You don't need to babysit me." Ian directed a flat, bored glance at Michael, then started shoving his food into a pile in the center of his plate. "I like being alone."

It hadn't always been the case. Before the accident…

Michael closed his eyes briefly, shutting away the

wave of guilt and sorrow that often caught him unaware.

At the sound of footsteps, he glanced over his
shoulder to find Janna carrying a fresh pot of coffee through the swinging half doors leading into
the kitchen.

Her daughter, a pretty little girl who was the image
of her mother with long, strawberry-blond hair and
a scattering of freckles across her nose, followed her
with a heaping bowl of colorful cereal held in both
hands. The child took her place at the table and
dropped her head in silent prayer.

Yet another way I've failed, he thought grimly. Ian
had often been angry and sullen since the accident,
blaming God and anyone who crossed his path for
his problems. Even now he rebelled against simple
meal time prayers.

"I thought you might like a little more caffeine,"
Janna said. Her gaze drifted to Ian after she topped
off Michael's coffee cup. "Is there something else I
can get for you? We've got…" She thought for a
moment, then nodded toward Rylie, her eyes twin-
kling. "My daughter's favorite marshmallow bits
cereal. Or leftover pizza."

His cheeks reddening, Ian shook his head.

She gave Michael a knowing look. "It takes a
while to settle in and feel comfortable, I know. Until
your cabin is ready, please do join us for all of your

meals, and if you get hungry for a snack in between, just track one of us down, okay?"

"Thanks." Michael cleared his throat and waited until Ian mumbled an awkward thanks, as well. "I've got to go into Wolf Creek today to meet with the mayor and town council. Ian is used to being on his own, though."

"He'll be fine." Janna's silky, strawberry-blond hair drifted against her cheek as she tilted her head and studied the boy thoughtfully. "I'll bet Rylie would like to show him around. There are lots of hiking trails in the area."

Rylie bounced in her chair, her ponytail swinging as she looked between Ian and Janna. "I even know where there's a stream with fish in it, and a cave. We could—"

Ian abruptly stood and pushed his chair away from the table.

"Ian!" His dad said.

"Leave me alone." Without another word, the boy limped out of the dining room and disappeared into the lobby.

Janna felt a wave of guilt as she watched him leave. "I am so sorry."

"He'll be okay." Michael shook his head slowly.

She saw a flash of grief on his face that he quickly masked with a wry smile. "I didn't even stop to think…"

"He's certainly capable of doing some hiking. He's just very self-conscious."

She paused, choosing her words carefully. "He… May I ask what happened?"

"A head-on collision." Setting aside his napkin, Michael rose abruptly, a muscle ticking along the side of his jaw. "Thanks for breakfast, ladies. It was delicious."

Janna watched him leave, her heart heavy. He clearly wanted to avoid any further questions, and she knew all too well about pain, sorrow and burdens that sometimes seemed too heavy to bear. Sometimes, however, it helped to talk about them.

"I'm sorry, Mom," Rylie breathed. "I didn't mean to make him feel sad."

"You didn't." Claire strolled into the dining room from the kitchen, a coffee cup in hand. At seventy-three she was still tall, straight and imperious, her leathery skin aged from decades of running a ranch on her own. "What's done is done, and there's no use whining about the past. Get over it and move on."

Words Janna had heard more times than she cared to count during her own childhood. Instead of counting to ten, she said a quick, silent prayer. *Please, Lord, give me the patience to deal with what I cannot change…and please, keep her from saying the wrong thing to that poor boy*. "Ian wasn't whining, Mom."

Claire snorted. "Self-pity never accomplished a

thing." She hovered at the table for a moment, then stalked away. "I'll be in my room."

Rylie blinked and swallowed hard. "Now even Grandma's mad," she whispered.

"Not at you, sweetheart."

"Because we moved here?"

"Because she needed to move in with us. Your grandmother is a proud woman, and it's hard for her to give up her independence." Janna rose and gave her daughter a hug. "I need to work on Cabin Five today, so Ian and his dad can move in. Maybe you could help me for a while. Later on you could offer Ian some ice cream…or see if he wants to borrow some movies."

"He doesn't like me." Rylie's lower lip trembled.

"That's not true at all, sweetie." Janna gave her a reassuring smile. "He just has some troubles that don't have anything to do with us, and that makes him sad. Maybe we can help him feel happier, if we try. Okay?"

The bleak expression in Rylie's eyes made Janna's heart twist. "That's what you said about Dad. And it never, ever worked."

After Rylie's heartbreaking words about her father, Janna spent an hour playing board games with her and working on a puzzle, then she brought Rylie and her dog out to the fenced playground by the lodge.

Within sight of Cabin Five, it was a pretty little

spot in the shade of the tall pines, with a swing set, slides, old-fashioned monkey bars and a huge sandbox with a baby pine tree now growing up through its center.

By midafternoon, Janna had managed to dismantle the rusted iron bed frames in the two bedrooms of Cabin Five and drag them out the back door, to join the filthy gray mattresses she'd wrestled into a hay wagon hitched to Claire's pickup.

The pile on the trailer had grown even higher by suppertime—broken chairs, a warped kitchen table and a couple of bedside tables that had been ruined by vermin, water damage and mold over the years.

Now, with the evening sun low in the sky, the last remnants of sunshine flooded through the west windows, highlighting the sparkling haze of dust she'd raised with a vigorous sweeping.

Footsteps crunched on twigs and gravel along the lane in front of the cabin, then someone knocked. The door hinges squealed. "Hello—anyone here?"

Startled by Michael's deep, masculine voice, Janna spun around toward the door, suddenly all too aware of how dingy the cabin looked right now. She could only imagine what he would think of his new lodgings, but it was too late. "H-hello. I'm afraid this isn't quite ready for inspection," she said with a nervous laugh. "But I promise you, it will look entirely different in a few days."

He stood in the center of the room and looked

around, a hint of a grin playing at the corners of his mouth. "I like it already. Reminds me of a place my uncle had—rustic but comfortable. Looks like it just needs a little dusting and some furniture."

She had to laugh at that. "You're sure easy to please."

"It's a great cabin." He braced his hands on a windowsill and stared at the mountains. The sun had slipped behind the peaks now, tinting the clouds in deep rosy hues with golden highlights. "It must be wonderful living here year-round, surrounded by God's glory. It's such a peaceful place."

Surprised and pleased to find that he was a man of faith, she smiled. But *peaceful* wasn't the first word that came to her mind—not with all the work to be done. "How did your first day on the job go? Anything wild happening in Wolf Creek?"

He glanced over his shoulder at her, a dimple deepening in his cheek. "Most exciting thing was the council meeting, I guess. They're concerned about how things are going while Sheriff Brownley is away."

"Concerned?"

"They needn't be." He turned and leaned a shoulder against the wall. Smiled. "With just two young officers on the force, they wanted someone with experience. That's why they brought me in for a year…though technically a sheriff needs to be elected."

Janna felt an unexpected flash of disappointment. "So you're temporary."

"Possibly. Figured I'd get settled here and work on

a fixer-upper house in my spare time, then keep it for vacations or sell at a profit in a few years. The way land prices are escalating, it could be a good investment." He shrugged. "But there's a good chance Brownley will opt for early retirement, so you never know."

From outside came the sound of Ian calling for his dad.

"I think you're being paged," Janna said with a smile.

Michael nodded and glanced around the cabin once more on his way to the door. "If you need help, just let me know. I put myself through college working construction."

"Thanks." The screen door closed with another squeal, then a murmur of deep voices faded away toward the lodge.

Suddenly feeling weary, she locked the back door, shut the windows and went out to stand on the front porch. Through the pines to the east, she could just make out the cheery lights of the lodge. To the west, the lane leading to the farthest cabins disappeared into the deepening shadows of the mountains. Mountains as familiar and beloved as old friends.

"How could I have stayed away all these years?" she murmured, rubbing her arms against the first hint of evening chill.

Something flickered through the trees past the last cabin. A flashlight?

Surely not.

It had to be a figment of her imagination. Michael and his son had headed for the lodge, and both Claire and Rylie were already inside for the night.

Weren't they?

She stepped back against the front of the cabin. Stared. Held her breath.

Something moved through the shadows and froze as if sensing discovery. Then it blended into the dusk and disappeared.

THREE

After a restless night of turbulent dreams, Janna awoke to the screeching of a hawk circling low over the lodge and the sound of a truck engine roaring to life. Dazed, she stumbled out of bed to the window and pulled up the shade.

Rivulets of rain on the glass turned the landscape into a watery, abstract image, though she could just make out the tailgate of Michael's truck disappearing down the lane. *Without breakfast*, she thought with a stab of guilt. And here it was—she glanced at her bedside clock—seven o'clock.

Shivering, she donned a set of gray sweats and thick socks and headed for the kitchen to start a pot of coffee.

The scent of fresh brew wafted from the kitchen when she walked in. A note of apology lay on the counter: "*Hope you don't mind—I made myself at home this morning.*"

She smiled sadly, wondering what it might have been like to have had a husband like Michael Robertson. Thoughtful. Obviously a steadfast and loving father, who was trying so hard to reach his troubled son.

A man who might have tried harder to make his marriage work and who wouldn't have drifted away, leaving a heartbroken daughter and unanswered questions in his wake.

Not that she was looking for husband number two, because that was one road she wouldn't be heading down again.

Her focus now was on the lodge. Her daughter. Keeping her elderly mother safe. And on Sunday, returning to the church home of her childhood…no matter how many eyebrows raised when she walked in the door.

Toenails clicked down the hall, and she looked down to see Maggie amble over and drop at her feet. The dog peered up at her through the fringe of white fur that arched over her eyes. "I suppose you need to go out, but I'll bet you aren't going to like it."

She crossed the kitchen to the back door and let the dog outside.

Maggie had always done a dynamite job of protecting the family from small, fur-bearing marauders—like chipmunks and squirrels that dared venture too close to the house—but she'd taken a cautious live-and-let-live approach with strangers.

She'd never been daring in inclement weather, either, preferring to do her business quickly so she could beg to be let back inside.

Janna straightened up the kitchen, then rubbed a wrist against the foggy window pane in the back door and squinted at the watery landscape. Strange. Where on earth was Maggie?

With all the rain, usually the little dog would have been back by now, desperately scratching at the door.

She opened the door and leaned out to call Maggie's name.

Nothing moved across the landscape. There was silence, save for the rain tapping on the porch roof and the rustle of leaves jostled by a fitful wind. Scents of wet earth and pine needles drifted inside.

Suddenly a small, bedraggled white form came bounding down the lane past Cabin One. "Good girl! Come on," Janna called out.

But Maggie didn't race to the door. She stopped just shy of the porch, then whirled around and bolted back up the lane, amidst a furious, nonstop volley of barking.

A foolish city dog could get in a *lot* of trouble if she wandered too far, given the coyotes, mountain lions and foxes in the area.

Shivering in the damp cold, Janna stepped out on the porch and hugged herself. "Maggie!"

The dog's stride didn't even falter, and a moment later she was out of sight.

Janna pulled on a slicker and a pair of rubber boots, then raced after her, still calling her name. Slipping and sliding on the rain-slickened gravel, Janna passed Cabins One, Two and Three.

Silly dog!

Cabin Four.

Out of breath, now, Janna slowed down. Would Maggie come back on her own? Maybe not—and moving to Wyoming had disrupted Rylie's life in too many ways to count without chancing the loss of her best friend. "Maggie!"

Cabins Five and Six flashed by.

The sound of barking grew louder.

Halfway up the hill to the last four cabins, she bent over with her hands on her knees and caught her breath. *Please, Lord. Don't let anything happen to Rylie's dog. Please!*

And then she saw it.

A shadowy figure perhaps a half mile ahead, moving rapidly away through the trees. In a flash he was gone, but Maggie didn't follow him. She froze for a split second, stared at the interloper, then veered off into the trees.

Janna followed the sound of her barking to the lip of a ravine beyond Cabin Ten and cautiously peered over the edge, hanging onto a slender birch for support.

Near the bottom Maggie barked furiously at something in the muddy earth. Probably some hapless chipmunk caught away from its burrow.

Janna coaxed. Pleaded. Called her name over and over. Then she finally made the descent, slipping on wet pine needles, tangling in thorny vines, while grabbing at bushes and branches to slow down.

"You are definitely getting a leash," Janna muttered when she finally made it to the bottom and reached for the muddy dog. Maggie desperately tried to wriggle free of her grasp, her paws peddling wildly. "And you definitely need a bath—"

But then Janna looked down and drew in a sharp breath.

Maggie hadn't been after a chipmunk at all.

Janna was now alone. Far from the lodge. No one knew she was out here—except for a stranger who might just be a hiker passing through…or who might care very much about what the dog had found.

A stranger who even now could be watching her from the shadows.

With a strangled cry she stumbled backward, the dog clutched at her chest—and stared at the eroded bank of the ravine…

Where Maggie had unearthed a human skull.

Shivering despite her shawl and dry clothes, Janna cradled a cup of coffee in both hands and gratefully absorbed its warmth.

Michael and one of his deputies had arrived less than an hour after she called 911—amazing, considering the twenty-mile distance from town on difficult mountain roads.

After telling them about the trespasser she'd seen in the woods and the strange, faded stains on Cabin Ten's floor, she'd led them to the place where she'd seen the skull, then went back to the lodge to stay out of their way.

They spent several hours out in the rain before the deputy drove away and Michael came back to the lodge.

Now he sat at the dining room table with Janna and Claire, his hand poised over a clipboard, the soft light of the rustic antler chandelier highlighting the angles and planes of his rugged face and deep, rain-damp waves in his dark hair.

If he was frustrated by Claire's imperious attitude, he certainly masked it well.

"So this place—the lodge and the cabins—have been empty for…"

Claire gave him a look of utter disdain. "The lodge, at least fifteen years. The cabins, much longer."

"The buildings were kept locked?"

"Of course."

"No one was allowed to use them? Family members? Friends?"

She took a long, slow sip of coffee. "The water and electricity were turned off, of course. I don't remember anyone…" Her brow furrowed. "Maybe a ranch hand used a cabin from time to time, while up here moving or doctoring cattle or riding fence. It's a long ways from the home place."

Michael's fingers tensed almost imperceptibly on his pen. "Would you still have records on your employees over the past, say, twenty years?"

Claire snorted. "There weren't that many." She lifted her gaze to the window beyond his shoulder, as if mentally cataloging each one. "Not more than a dozen. I always kept detailed records on everything pertaining to the ranch, but those files are at the ranch office, not here."

He tilted his head slightly, studying her. "I don't suppose you did prehire background checks."

That earned a sharp, derisive laugh. "In these parts, a few phone calls are enough."

Janna nodded. "Word travels fast in a small town, and the ranchers know each other well. If someone was fired for good reason, he probably wouldn't find another job in the entire county." Janna frowned as Michael's words registered. "You said twenty years. Are you guessing the bones have been here that long?"

He lifted a shoulder. "I don't even want to hazard a guess, but we'll probably have some preliminary answers for you once the state crime lab people get out here."

"The *state*?" Claire's chin jerked up. "You can't deal with this on your own?"

"We need to call in some experts. Our county can't afford its own forensics specialists or a crime lab."

"They can't go traipsing all over, digging and ruining my land," Claire snapped.

"No, it's nothing like that," Michael said with a reassuring smile. "The director will send out a team—just a single van—and they'll process the scene in a single day. Possibly tomorrow or Thursday." He shifted his attention to Janna. "You'll barely know they're here, unless they need to ask you some questions."

Even from across the table, Janna could see a vein pulsing at her mother's temple, a sure sign of her rising anger. Anger that had always been quick to ignite, but now—coupled with the doctor's strong suspicions about early Alzheimer's—it was far more unpredictable and intense.

Janna lifted a brow and pointedly slid a glance toward Claire, then met Michael's gaze, hoping he'd catch her silent message. "Perhaps you could tell us a little more about what these investigators will be doing, Michael. Just so there aren't any…surprises?"

A corner of his mouth lifted. "The team will take measurements and create diagrams of the scene, then they'll carefully excavate the burial site, looking for evidence. They'll probably take a lot of video footage and dozens—even hundreds—of digital photos to show the position of anything they find."

"And the remains?"

"Those will go back to the crime lab, along with anything else that can be analyzed. Maybe forensics can help identify the deceased and figure out the cause of death."

Claire drummed her fingers on the table. "And how long does that take?"

"Quite a while, I'm afraid. The lab has to prioritize its workload based on which cases are scheduled for court, and whether or not immediate suspects are being held. A cold case like this one will take a backseat."

"Weeks?"

"Probably many months. Worst-case scenario, maybe a year or more. Real life isn't exactly like what you see on TV."

Janna worried at her lower lip. "But we could soon face a flood of reporters."

"The local paper, if they get wind of what's going on," he admitted. "Wider coverage, if we actually bring someone to trial. But that's jumping the gun, given how long those bones have been here. And supposing that we eventually do identify the killer, he might even be deceased himself by now."

"We'll cooperate with you, of course." Janna eyed her mother's rigid jaw. "Won't we?"

Claire's mouth thinned, though she gave a faint nod.

Michael dropped his pen on the table and leaned back in his chair, the picture of affable charm. "So, what do you think?" His casual air belied the sharp intensity in his eyes. "Anyone from the past come to mind—any difficult employees?"

"If they were difficult, they packed their bags. I had no time for boozers or fighters. Not with three girls to raise and a ranch to run."

Michael toyed idly with the handle of his coffee cup. "Remember any local troublemakers over the years? Neighbors…trespassers…any suspicious activity in the area?"

"No." Claire gathered her cup and saucer and stood. "So are we done here?"

Michael rose, as well, and nodded. "If there's anything else, I can always check with you later. In the meantime, Janna can probably answer some of my questions."

Claire's dismissive gaze flicked toward Janna. "She deserted this ranch a long time ago, so I doubt that very much."

"What about your other daughters?"

"Leigh's doing a vet school residency but she's moving back in the fall," Claire snapped. "You can find Tessa working down at the ranch or up in the mountains. I never know where."

Michael waited until Claire left the room, then settled back in his chair. "Sorry. I didn't mean to open any old wounds."

"It's okay. My mother and I have a rather long and difficult history." Janna hesitated, weighing her mother's rights to privacy against the added security of having another adult aware of the situation. "Since you're staying at the lodge, you should probably know that her doctor suspects early Alzheimer's."

"That's hard for both of you, I'm sure," he said, his voice warm with sympathy.

"One reason my daughter and I came back to Wyoming was to help my sisters care for her, but she isn't very happy about it. She's a proud and independent woman." Janna studied the remaining coffee in her cup. "About your questions…my sisters and I were in our early teens during the time frame you mentioned. I don't recall anything unusual."

"No exciting local headlines? Scandals or rumors about missing people?"

"If there had been, this town would've been abuzz with curiosity." Janna shrugged. "The hottest gossip of the day was the affair between the postmistress and the owner of a tavern in the next town. They carried on for years and probably never realized that the whole town knew."

"And your mother's ranch hands?"

Janna smiled wryly. "As soon as we girls could ride, we were pretty much it. I was the bookworm and never as good a cowgirl as Tessa and Leigh, but we all racked up a lot of wet saddle blankets over the years. Mom usually had just one, maybe two men working for her. Most came and went pretty fast, though, because she wasn't easy to work for. I can see about finding their files."

"It's possible the body was simply dumped here—maybe even hauled from a great distance in an effort to hide it well. But I want to check every local angle." Michael dropped his pen into the pocket of his shirt. "In the meantime, be sure to remind everyone to stay away from the area cordoned off with yellow caution tape. Tomorrow, too."

"No problem." She shivered. "I just want this to be over as soon as possible."

* * *

Ian and Rylie had been ordered to stay inside the lodge, but with each new vehicle that pulled in the next morning, Ian grew more impatient.

"I wouldn't be in the way," he growled as he watched two uniformed women step out of a Wyoming State patrol car. "Only cool thing all summer, and I'm supposed to stay inside like some kindergartner."

"It's a crime scene," Janna repeated. "I'm sure your dad will tell you all he can later on."

Rylie hugged herself, her eyes widening. "What if the murderer is still here?"

"He probably is," Ian retorted with obvious relish. "He might even be a serial killer, and—"

"Ian!" Janna gave him a look that could have stopped a freight train, but he just shrugged and looked unrepentant.

"Stands to reason. Abandoned resort…an isolated place. A guy could ditch a lot of bodies out here, and no one would ever know."

"That's *enough*." She pointed toward the stairs. "If you're bent on scaring a little girl, then you need to spend some time by yourself."

He grumbled something under his breath, but gave up his post at the windows and flopped onto one of the leather couches by the fireplace.

Rylie burrowed into Janna's arms. "Maybe Ian's right. That man could be outside right now, waiting for us."

"You're safe, sweetheart." Janna lifted her gaze to the fireplace, where she could just barely see the top of Ian's head. "And if anyone tries to tell you differently, you come to me. Okay?"

But even as she reassured her daughter, Janna had her own doubts. There'd definitely been a trespasser on the property, two days in a row. And even from a distance the guy had seemed furtive. Nervous.

Maybe he was just a random hiker, who had no idea of the mystery unfolding at the resort. Maybe there'd even been a different person, the second time. But what if he was after something here—or even knew something about the person who'd gone missing long ago?

The coincidental timing made it seem possible, and that thought sent a chill down Janna's spine.

The early mist had burned away by midmorning, and by noon the sun blazed overhead. It was early evening before the crime lab team drove away and Michael came back to the lodge, his uniform mud stained and his face weary.

Janna met him on the porch of the lodge with an ice-cold glass of tea. "You look exhausted," she said.

He gratefully accepted the glass and downed the icy liquid in several long swallows. "The others worked straight through because they've got another crime scene tomorrow. So I did, too."

"Any clues yet?"

"Nothing definitive." He glanced down at the

damp, newly bathed dog at his feet. "The spring runoff was especially high this year, which is probably why Maggie was able to find most of the remains. If not for her, they might never have been found."

Janna glanced back toward the house and lowered her voice. *"Most?"*

"It's hard to say when the burial site was first disturbed. If it was early on, coyotes or wolves might've made off with some of it. We did a thorough search and the crime lab even brought in a dog, but we didn't find a complete skeleton."

Feeling faint, Janna backed up to an Adirondack chair and sat down. "Was there enough to help you find out who it was?"

"We recovered part of the skull—enough for dental records, so we've got a start. And…" He hesitated, clearly keeping some of the details to himself. "We found items in the vicinity that may help narrow down the approximate year of death."

"What happens next?"

"I'll search old records for missing persons. Newspaper archives."

"What about DNA?"

Michael rubbed his jaw. "These days, DNA samples would be collected from a missing person's home and kept indefinitely to help with identification. Toothbrushes. Strands of hair. But at the probable time of this death, that technology was still fairly new and there wasn't a national database. Still, we can make a positive ID if there are any records on file—more likely, if the victim had a criminal past."

"Can you tell us what you find out?"

Michael shook the ice in his glass, clearly debating what to say as he surveyed the mountain peaks. "In time."

"Can you at least tell me if it was a murder?"

"Obviously, this was a burial, not just someone who keeled over in the woods." He looked over his shoulder at her, his eyes pensive. "But was it premeditated? The result of a fight or a moment of anger? Maybe the poor guy took a hard fall…or committed suicide and his buddy panicked, afraid he'd be blamed. We'll know more when we get the report back from the DCI."

"But you did see a probable cause of death."

Michael turned and leaned against the porch rail, his thumbs hooked in his front jeans pockets. "Possible, not definite. But I wouldn't get my hopes up too high, because a lot of cold cases are never solved. If the bones belong to some drifter, perhaps a missing persons report was never filed."

She shivered and wrapped her arms around herself, imagining what might have happened on this property—the terror and pain. Had there been a desperate fight for survival, or had the victim been caught unaware? "Would you have just a ballpark estimate on when it happened? I keep wondering if his killer could still be on the loose around here."

Michael hesitated. "From items found at the site, we know it didn't happen before 1990, but the DCI will have more definitive answers later."

Janna's breath caught in her throat as she thought back. She'd been sixteen that year. Throughout high school she and her sisters had ridden in this area often, to move cattle to summer range or for impromptu picnics with the Langley girls from the neighboring ranch. If she and the others had come by at the wrong moment and had seen too much...

"...but don't talk about anything you've seen or heard regarding this case—not even with your family," Michael continued. "No sense in letting word spread and alerting any possible suspects, right?"

She pulled her thoughts back to the present. "No. Of course not. Did you find any signs of the man I saw on our property?"

Michael shook his head. "The rain probably helped cover his tracks. You couldn't see any identifying features?"

"Not even what he was wearing, really—given the distance. It just looked like he was wearing a dark hooded jacket of some kind." Janna pensively gnawed at her lower lip. "But maybe he was a hiker who happened to be in the area. Just a coincidence, maybe."

"Perhaps."

But a coincidence didn't seem likely, and given the look in Michael's eyes, he felt the same way. "So what's next?"

"We'll eventually get a DCI report on the victim, and they'll also be testing the stains on the floor in Cabin Ten for DNA. In the meantime, I'll be looking into old missing-persons reports and unsolved crimes in the area." He glanced at his watch. "Speaking of that, I'd better get going. The dispatcher called me a few minutes ago about some break-ins on the other side of the county. Will you all be okay?"

"Actually...I need to go to town for my mother's prescriptions, and I have an appointment with my lawyer. Is it okay if we leave?"

"Everything's under control here. If we have any further questions, they can wait until you get back." He started for the door, then hesitated. "Just be careful, okay? If the killer is still in the area, he isn't going to be happy about this discovery."

All the way to town, Janna was lost in thought. Until now, she'd seen only the "civilian" side of Michael.

The moment he arrived after her 911 call, he'd seemed like a different man. His professional persona with his officers and their obvious respect for him had instantly piqued her curiosity. What could have brought a man like him to this small, backwater town, when he was obviously so adept at his career?

Janna pulled into a parking space in front of the only drugstore in town. She rested her head briefly on the top curve of the steering wheel, the enormity and horror of the day's events settling over her like a damp, suffocating blanket.

Before moving here, she'd expected hard work and an ongoing struggle to bring the lodge back to life. She hadn't expected a death, investigators and possible danger.

As she stepped out of the truck, she felt the hairs at the back of her neck prickle. She stopped. Looked around.

A middle-aged cowboy leaned against the door of a battered pickup just a dozen feet away. The narrowed look he gave her was laced with pure venom. "Like living alone, do you?" His voice was low, deadly. "Just you and that daughter of yours, and the old lady?"

He was a complete stranger, but the threat in his voice was unmistakable. She stared back at him in disbelief. "Wh-who are you?"

His laugh was sharp, without humor. "Don't matter none, now does it? Especially not to a high-and-mighty McAllister."

She bit back a sharp reply. High and mighty? If only he knew. Forcing herself to ignore him, she turned away to walk into the drugstore, though she felt his glare burning into her back.

When she glanced over her shoulder, he was gone.

FOUR

"I don't see anyone out there now." Wade Hollister tipped the blinds down with a forefinger and peered out the front window of his law office, his lips pursed. "What did the guy look like?"

"Middle-aged, probably. An old, silver-belly gray western hat. Leathery skin. Maybe a little over six feet." Janna shifted uncomfortably on the wooden chair, thankful that she'd dropped Rylie and Claire off for a visit at her sister Tessa's place before coming into town. "He didn't threaten me, exactly, but he sure seemed to relish the fact that my mother, daughter and I are living out at the lodge on our own."

"Your description of him fits half the cowboys in this county, Janna. Did you see what kind of truck he had?"

"Dusty. Beat up. A dark color—black, I think."

"And that describes about half the trucks. Maybe it isn't such a good idea, you being so far from town." Wade released the metal blinds and turned toward her with a frown. "Two women and a child alone."

She waved away his concern. "We aren't."

"I'm not sure your lodge guests would be much protection, my dear."

"Our first one sure is." Janna sorted through the manila folder in her lap and withdrew a draft of a lease contract for Snow Canyon Lodge. "Can't beat an interim sheriff."

"He's not there all the time though, is he?"

"No, but soon we'll have a constant parade of guests, which ought to dissuade anyone from causing trouble. Too many eyes." She held out the document. "My mother and I discussed your latest version last night. We're ready to sign, once we have a final copy."

Wade settled into the leather executive chair behind a mahogany desk that dominated his modest office space before leisurely reaching across the polished surface to accept it. "You're sure you don't want to wait awhile? Just to make sure this is the right decision?"

"It is."

"Even though it locks you into a ten-year contract?"

"*With* the right to renew for the same time period, and to buy that part of the Snow Canyon Ranch property."

Janna remembered Wade from her high school days, when he'd been a young history teacher fresh out of college.

Though he'd been a nice guy, he'd been an uninspired instructor, and after that first year he left town and went to law school.

Maybe that distant association made him feel like her mentor, but at the age of thirty-three she wanted help with legal matters, not fatherly advice.

Moving an ashtray aside, he braced his elbows on the desk and steepled his fingertips. "That murder investigation isn't going to be good for business."

Startled, she met his gaze.

"Don't be surprised," he said with a chuckle. "This area doesn't exactly have the latest dispatch system technology. The locals can entertain themselves by eavesdropping with their scanners. I heard the call, and I expect half the people in the county did, too."

Michael's parting words now sent a shiver through her. *"The killer might not be too happy about this discovery."* What if he was still somewhere in the area and had already heard about it?

She lifted her jaw to show confidence she didn't quite feel. "There's no proof it was a murder."

"That's not what I gathered from my scanner. Your friend has already called in the Wyoming DCI."

"True…but I understand it was sort of a formality." She shrugged. "I don't imagine they'll ever find out anything, and the case certainly has nothing to do with the lodge itself."

"You're sure of that?" He pursed his lips. "Stands to reason that someone from your mother's ranch was involved, given the isolated location. A hot-headed ranch hand, maybe. Who else would have access to that area?"

The direction of the conversation made her uneasy. "Maybe it was someone just passing through. An accident or something. Look, about that contract—"

"The lodge is a risky investment," Wade said firmly, ignoring her attempt to change the topic. "A fledgling business, negative publicity—you're falling into a bad situation, Janna."

"What makes me feel worse is the poor person who died. We'll probably never find out who it was, but what about the family? Do they still wonder about his or her disappearance? Or did they die heartbroken because they never found out what happened?"

"I understand your feelings." Wade sighed. "I'm just trying to look at all of this from a business point of view. This discovery was unfortunate timing. But with luck, maybe you can keep the local media quiet."

"Our Web site will draw vacationers from across the country, not Wolf Creek. I hardly think they'll be reading our local newspaper."

"True." He tapped a pen against his desk blotter. "One other thing—do you know much it will cost to bring the place up to code?"

"I plan to do a lot of the work myself. And thanks to my inheritance from Uncle Gray, I should be okay as long as I can start bringing in guests by midsummer."

"As I remember, his estate was split between you and your sisters, so I hope you're right." Wade smiled gently. "Understand that as your lawyer, I'm just trying to protect your interests. Bankruptcy is not a pretty experience."

"I'll be fine." But her stomach tightened. Was Wade right? Was she risking everything she owned on an investment that would fail? *Please, Lord, guide me. I need to help my mother and support my daughter— am I doing the right thing?* "So…can we finish up this contract?"

"As you wish." He gazed down at the contract, his eyes narrowed as he scanned the notes she'd written in the margins. "I do think we could find some loopholes here, should you change your mind later."

"Loopholes, in a contract with my *mother?*" Janna sat back in her chair, appalled.

Wade's mouth lifted in a wry grin. "I'm afraid you wouldn't believe how difficult family relationships can be. Should you find that you've made a mistake, would you really want to be tied to that crumbling old lodge for another ten years?"

"If I'd given my word, yes." Janna looked at her watch. "Look, I'd better get going. Can you give me a call when the contract is ready?"

"No problem." Bracing a hand on his desk, he rose halfway out of his chair for a hearty handshake. "End of this week, easily. And about that man you saw out on the street…" His brow furrowed. "I'd be careful, if I were you. Your mother made some enemies in these parts, over the years. Some people might even think…"

"That she was involved in that murder?" Horrified, Janna stood and gave him a level look. "That's ridiculous."

He tipped his head in agreement. "Of course it is. And as far as her ranch is concerned, I know she only did what she thought best, but over the years she stepped on some toes in the process."

"If she were a man, she'd simply be considered a successful rancher. Why wouldn't she make sound business decisions?"

Wade splayed out his hands in a placating gesture. "I fully agree with you. Claire McAllister is one shrewd woman, and she deserved her success. But unfortunately, you won't find that she has many friends in these parts."

Janna instinctively wanted to argue and defend her mother, but she'd grown up here and knew he was speaking the truth. "Maybe so, but that's something I can't fix right now. Just let me know when I can pick up the contracts."

When she stepped out the front door, Main Street was empty save for a few dusty pickups parked in front of the tiny grocery store at the end of the block.

Still, she felt the eerie sensation that someone was watching her.

She glanced back at Wade's office, then studied the storefronts on both sides of the streets. Scanned the shadows of the pines at both ends of two-block-long business district.

There was no one in sight.

Setting her jaw, she strode to her pickup with all the confidence she could muster. Maybe Wade was right, but whatever the local opinions were, she'd come here to start a new life for herself and her daughter.

And no matter what anyone said, that's what she was going to do.

Four days in Wyoming, and he was already bored out of his mind.

Ian flipped through a magazine. Tossed it on a growing stack of discards by his bed, then rolled over on his back and stared at the pine-paneled ceiling of his room which had twelve knotholes, including one that bore a striking resemblance to his grandma Mary. The lodge sucked.

No TV reception.

He'd left the power cord to his PlayStation at home.

And other than the crabby old lady who'd glared at him over breakfast, the woman who ran the place, and her little brat, there probably wasn't another person for fifty miles. A hundred.

He might as well be stuck in jail…and the irony of the whole situation almost made him want to cry, because maybe that's where he deserved to be.

With a gut-deep sigh, he levered himself off the bed and pulled on his shabby Nikes. He thundered down the lodge staircase and burst out the front door to the wide, sweeping covered porch. A pair of chipmunks scattered down the steps at his approach.

He knew how to bridle a horse. Maybe he could just hop on that old gray one and take it for a spin, and no one would be the wiser.

He felt his shoulders slump under the weight of the consequences if Dad found out about *that.* Ever since the accident, he'd been coddled and watched over like a three-year-old kid, and there was no way Dad would miss the telltale sign of a stray horse hair somewhere. Sometimes Dad just *knew* things—like he had ESP or something. And he'd made Ian promise to stay close to the lodge until the investigation was over.

A lane led through the pines and up a hill toward the cabins, where at least he might be able to explore a little. His heart lifted at the thought of seeing wildlife or maybe finding some old arrowheads.

He'd made it to the farthest cabin before he gave in to the stiffness and pain in his leg and had to sit down on a log to take long, slow breaths, his eyes squeezed shut.

Quick little footsteps hurried up the road, and a second later, Rylie plopped down on the log next to him.

Her eyes were alive with curiosity when she smiled up at him, and he steeled himself for the inevitable questions.

The questions that had made him want to avoid school forever…because there he was a curiosity. A freak. Even to the guys he'd known before the wreck.

"My mom is working on your cabin," she announced cheerfully. "Are you glad to be here?"

Glad? It was so far from the truth that he felt his mouth curl into a derisive snarl. "Oh, yeah. Really."

She pulled back a little, her eyebrows drawing together. "It's pretty here."

He rolled his eyes but didn't answer, hoping she'd take the hint and go away.

"And your cabin is really nice inside. Mom says—"

He stood abruptly, ignoring the pain that knifed through his knee at the sudden motion and the brief haze of black spots that danced in front of his eyes.

Rylie was still at his heels when he stepped over the barricade of pine logs lying across the lane, just beyond the last cabin. "Are you going hiking? There's some trails up there. One even goes to a waterfall. It's really fun. My mom and me really like to…"

Ignoring her chatter and a small, insistent voice of warning in his head, he skirted the area marked with yellow crime-scene tape and kept going.

Dad had made him promise to stay close to the lodge until the murder investigation was complete. Ian had given his word. But now he forced himself to lengthen his stride until the trail grew steeper and he could no longer hear Rylie tagging along behind him. He suppressed the impulse to look back, knowing that he was mean and small to treat her this way, but needing to be alone, whatever the cost.

Because he knew exactly what would happen.

It was only a matter of time before she'd start peppering him with questions about the burn scars on his face. The gnarled scars snaking down his arm. The way he had to clench a pen in his fist like some preschooler and the way he limped like some old man. And then she'd get all wide-eyed and ask about the accident, and that would be worse.

Even after retelling the story a thousand times, it still had the power to tighten his stomach into a fierce knot and send waves of lava-hot guilt through his heart.

Far up the trail, he staggered to an exhausted stop, the altitude and the exertion robbing him of breath. He sagged against a boulder. When his breathing slowed, he caught the distant sound of rushing water. Rylie's waterfall?

Intrigued, he forced himself to continue up the rocky path and through a heavy stand of pines.

And there it was—sparkling like a cascade of crystals falling from a cliff high above. Splashing into a dark, mossy pool rimmed with boulders, as if a giant had placed each of them in perfect symmetry. At the far end of the pool, the water flowed into a stream that disappeared into the trees.

Ian's breath caught. Across the water, nearly hidden in the shadows, a bulky form stirred, twisted around and froze—looking straight at him. A *bear?*

Fear lanced through him. He was alone, at least a mile from the lodge. No one but Riley knew he was out here. No one would know exactly where to look.

And there was no way he could run fast enough to reach safety.

He eased back a step, then another, never taking his eyes away from the hulking creature, his heartbeat thundering in his ears.

He blinked. Squinted, and then felt his tension ease. It wasn't a bear. Now that his eyes had adjusted to the shadows, he could make out the shape of someone with a backpack and a bulky jacket, though the distance was too great to make out the guy's features. He seemed to be searching for something on the ground.

His knees rubbery with relief, Ian started to raise a hand in greeting. But the man feverishly gathered some objects at his feet, then he spun around and disappeared into the trees.

Weird.

Ian stayed motionless for several minutes, his thoughts flying through a dozen possibilities. Maybe the guy was on the run. An escapee from prison. The murderer. Or a bank robber. Or some crazy guy who lived in the woods.

Just a camper, more likely. Someone who wanted to enjoy nature all alone.

Snorting in disgust at his initial fear, Ian made his way to the pool of water and peered into its dark and mysterious depths, imagining the wild prehistoric creatures that could be living down there.

On the other side, something glinted in a thin shaft of sunlight.

Curious, he scrambled over the rocks to where the stranger had been. He searched the thick bed of pine needles, his frustration rising. There was nothing, except a crumpled ball of aluminum foil. No exciting treasures, after all. The jerk had simply been eating his lunch, probably, then dropped the foil on the ground.

Disappointed, Ian turned to leave, picking up the foil as an afterthought. His fingers disturbed a thin layer of pine needles and brushed against something cold.

It was a pocket knife. He grinned and lifted it for inspection. The case was heavily tarnished, but it was still pretty cool—three blades, plus a corkscrew and all sorts of tools on the opposite side. He looked around, ready to shout after the man who'd left. But there was absolute silence, except for the rush of the waterfall. Not a leaf stirred.

A bone-deep chill worked its way down his spine as he took in the menacing shadows of trees that seemed to press in on him from every side. The darkening clouds that were barely visible over the heavy canopy of branches overhead. A twig snapped…then another.

Suddenly he knew—without a shred of doubt—that staying here a minute longer would be a terrible mistake.

Ignoring the leg muscles that screamed in protest, he pivoted and started running—raced over the tumble of rocks around the pool and fled down the path, slipping and sliding on loose pebbles and pine needles until his lungs were raw and aching and the cabins finally came into view. He collapsed on the steps of the first one he reached, his heart pounding and muscles quivering.

Had he heard a harsh curse the moment he'd started to run? Had there been someone just behind him? Maybe it had all just been his imagination, born of too many Stephen King books read late at night.

Then he uncurled his fingers and stared at the knife in his palm. He hadn't thought to drop it. Maybe the owner was the guy he'd seen—and would follow him here, irate and accusing Ian of theft. If he told Dad…

Ian's stomach lurched.

He absently rubbed at the drab, outside case of the knife, wondering what to say. A sharp beam of sunlight lasered up into his face from the spot he'd just cleaned, where the metal now gleamed like molten silver.

Holding his breath, he carefully snagged one of the blades open with the edge of a fingernail.

Though the case might be real silver, the blade was badly rusted, and flakes of brownish residue blew away on the cool breeze. Disappointment washed through him. It was just a stupid old knife—probably lost for years and years—though at least he didn't have to worry about that creepy guy coming after it.

Disgusted, he nearly dropped it to the ground… but then had a sudden thought.

Who knew? There were faint initials on it—not clear enough to read. But maybe it had belonged to a fur trapper. Or even an explorer. If it was *really* old, maybe he could try selling it on eBay.

His spirits lifting, he shoved it deep in his jeans pocket and sauntered down to Cabin Five.

Dad still might be mad about him going off on a hike, though, so he wouldn't say anything about it just yet.

After all, what could be the harm in that?

FIVE

Michael parked his patrol car in the shade of several towering pines by the lodge and sauntered up the walk. Just as he'd expected, Ian was slumped in a porch swing at the far end of the porch. Alone, and appearing completely bored.

The boy didn't even bother to look up when Michael dropped into a weathered wicker chair next to the swing. "So…did you have any fun today?"

Ian angled a brief look at him that suggested Michael was insane, then silently slouched even lower.

"Play video games?"

Silence.

"Watch any movies?"

No answer.

"Read?"

He *wanted* to ask if Ian had pulled out the new charcoals and sketch pads Michael had casually left in his room after work on Thursday, but knew it was a dangerous topic to broach.

The physical therapists back home had worked with Ian for months, trying to bring back some of his old dexterity. Encouraging him to begin drawing again, however laborious.

After a few awkward attempts, Ian had thrown the art materials against the wall in a rage, and with them, every hope of regaining his artistic gifts.

Before, he'd fought his pain, pushing himself to the limit in therapy to regain his strength and agility. But since that failure, he'd fallen into a dark and moody place where attempts to reach him were often met with surly defiance.

Michael tried another tack. "So, did you check with Janna about horseback riding?"

Ian lifted a shoulder.

"Janna said you could ride Frosty around here, if you'd like." He found it easier to interrogate a suspect than to initiate a conversation with his son when Ian wasn't in the mood, and the good times were few and far between these days. "Didn't she say her sister would be back from a pack trip on Saturday? We'll have to go on some long trail rides."

A faint tinge of pink rose in the boy's face. "Whatever."

Realization dawned, too late. "You know, we wouldn't go far—just an hour or so. If you were comfortable, then we'd go a lot longer the next—"

"Don't treat me like some cripple," Ian snarled. He vaulted awkwardly out of the porch swing, staggered at the sudden weight thrust onto his bad leg and caught himself against the porch railing. "Just leave me *alone*."

Michael automatically launched forward to help him, then froze, knowing it would only make matters worse if he interfered. "Ian—"

"No, Dad," Ian bit out. "I don't need your help."

He straightened, squared his shoulders and managed to affect a casual saunter the length of the porch, then disappeared into the lodge, letting the screen door swing shut behind him with a resounding *smack.*

Michael rubbed his face, then leaned forward and rested his forehead against his palm as guilt, coupled with a deep sense of failure, settled in his midsection.

The screen door squealed, and he looked up to find Janna approaching with two tall glasses.

She walked to the end of the porch and handed him one, then leaned a hip against the porch and saluted him with the other. "You look like a man who could use a good, stiff iced tea."

"You overheard?"

"No, but I saw him stomp through the lobby and go up to his room. He looked upset." She tilted her head toward the windows looking out onto the porch. "And then I noticed you were out here."

"Just another successful conversation," he said wearily. He took a long, slow swallow of tea. "One of many that have ended exactly the same way."

"It has to be tough."

"The poor kid's life totally changed the day of the

accident. He's been through more surgeries and more pain than anyone should have to bear."

"And it has to be awfully tough on you, too."

Surprised, Michael looked up and found her eyes warm and understanding. "I'm not the one who got hurt."

"But I know you feel every bit of his pain, and that it has to be tough dealing with his emotional issues." A corner of her mouth lifted in a wry smile. "I remember all too well how stormy teen years can be. Coupled with everything else, well…I know it can't be easy. I think you're doing a great job with him."

Her words bit deep. "Tell that to his grandparents."

"Are they…quite involved?"

"You mean overbearing?" He closed his eyes briefly against the memory of their most recent visit. "No. They mean well. They're good people. If they could, they'd wrap him in cotton wool and never let him out of their sight. Since Elise died…well, Ian is all they have of her now."

Janna drew in a sharp breath. "I'm so sorry. I didn't realize."

"My wife and I separated three years ago. I tried to reconcile many times, but…" He hesitated, wanting to honor her memory despite the fact that she'd certainly never honored her own marriage vows. "She wanted more in life than to be the wife of a homicide detective, and I suppose I can't blame her for that."

Janna rubbed at the condensation on her glass with a thumb. "Poor Ian…and you, too. How did she die?"

He'd known the question would come up, sooner or later, but as many times as he'd had to answer it, he still felt his throat thicken and his heart wrench over what Ian would have to carry for the rest of his life.

"The car accident."

"Oh, no…" Janna's eyes widened. "Not with your son."

"He was at the wheel. A drunk driver crossed the median and hit them head-on. The other driver and Elise died instantly. Ian was in a coma for several days—a blessing in some ways, I guess."

"In some ways?"

"He remembers nothing about the horrific details of the accident…doesn't have to live with the memory of seeing his mother at the scene." Michael swallowed. "On the other hand, he refuses to believe that he couldn't have avoided the abrupt, erratic action of the other driver."

"That poor boy," Janna breathed, her face etched with sorrow. She reached out to take Michael's hand, the warm and gentle touch conveying her compassion. "I just don't know what to say."

"The irony is that it wasn't Ian's fault—it was mine." The pain was always there—despite prayers for forgiveness, and countless prayers for the ability to let go of the past. Even now that pain tightened like a vise around his heart. "Elise and I did not agree on much, including what was best for Ian. I thought she was too controlling. She thought I let him do too much. When she said she didn't want him to drive, I figured she was just being difficult about that, too. What boy doesn't count the days until he can get his permit? So I insisted that she let him…and then I bought him a car."

"Oh, Michael." Janna's voice filled with sympathy. "Most kids learn to drive, but nothing like this happens to them. The accident was not your fault."

"There you're wrong. Because I was stubborn, Ian's mom and the other driver died. And my son will live with guilt for the rest of his life."

"Obnoxious boy. If that boy was mine, he would've learned a thing or two about manners and respect by now." Claire stood in the door of Cabin Five, her arms folded across her chest. Her gaze was fixed on Janna, and from the glint in her eye, Janna guessed her mother was recalling some of their more memorable arguments during Janna's teen years.

Exasperated, Janna said her fourth silent prayer for patience since breakfast. "He's had troubles in his life, Mom. He needs love and understanding."

"What he needs is a firm hand to the backside. You haven't heard him talk back to his dad? That's what I would've done."

"Hmm." Janna made a vague gesture with her hand

but kept polishing a grimy window, knowing that any argument would just release the floodgates for more complaints.

Two down, five windows to go, and then she could start hanging some cheerful gingham curtains. After hours of work, she felt true satisfaction at seeing the place begin to sparkle. *Concentrate on the positive*, she reminded herself.

Claire took a step into the entryway and planted her hands on her hips. "I wouldn't worry too much about turning this place into a palace—maybe he and his dad will move on."

Janna laughed. "This will never be a palace, Mom. It's a very rustic cabin. But it has to be clean and comfortable, and when the Robertsons move out of the lodge, you won't have to see them as much."

"Humph." Claire ran a finger along the top of the refrigerator and inspected it for grime. "You didn't clean this."

Janna sighed. "It has to be replaced, actually. I found a nice used one in the want ads. It'll be delivered later today along with a newer stove."

"Too much money. Way too much money you're putting into this foolish idea. You never did have any business sense—not with that nose of yours in those books all the time. Now Tessa—she knew how to put in a hard day's work." Claire's eyes gleamed with satisfaction. "A good gal, my Tessa."

Janna fought the urge to knock her forehead against

the wall in sheer frustration. "Yes, she is. And she's coming over this morning, remember? She said she'd take you back to the home place for the day, if you'd like to go."

Confusion and fear clouded Claire's eyes, followed by the inevitable flash of anger. "You didn't tell me that," she snapped. "Why not?"

Tessa had talked to Claire on the phone yesterday, but reminding her would probably just upset her more. "I'm sorry...I must have forgotten," Janna said gently. "Do you want to go?"

"Of course I do. That's where I should be, after all. I don't belong here."

"You'll be going just for the afternoon, Mom. Tessa is gone for weeks at a time on her pack trips, and she's also busy with the livestock, so you wouldn't have any company if you lived there. Maybe next winter, when things slow down for her..."

Claire's eyes sparked with fire at the reminder. "I was born in that house and so were you girls. I lived there for seventy-two years, and I hardly need *company* watching over me."

Unable to come up with a tactful answer to that, Janna finished polishing the window, then put the plastic bucket of cleaning supplies on the kitchen table.

Given Claire's declining health, the best options had been to consider supervised residential care, find an in-home caretaker, or have her live with a daughter who could watch over her consistently. As always, the three sisters had vehemently disagreed, but in the end they'd finally come to a consensus.

With Tessa's schedule and Leigh not moving back to the area until later in the year, Janna had been the best option. Unfortunately, she and Claire had always shared the stormiest mother-daughter relationship.

At the sound of truck tires crunching up the lane, she breathed a sigh of relief. "I think that's Tessa now."

Instantly Claire's face transformed. Without a word, she pivoted and strode out of the cabin.

"I love you, too, Mom," Janna whispered softly as she took a last look around the cabin, then shut the door and followed Claire up to the lodge.

Tessa leaned against her truck, her McAllister strawberry-blond hair pulled through the back of a ball cap in a long ponytail, her T-shirt revealing sun-bronzed, well-toned arms. The pair of leather gloves hanging out of the back pocket of her worn jeans suggested that she'd just finished working a horse or fixing fence, and that her day was far from finished.

Trim, athletic and strictly no-nonsense about her appearance, Tessa had an air of intelligent competence that Janna had always admired.

Claire went straight for the passenger-side door and climbed in, but Tessa pushed away from the truck and met Janna partway. As usual, she cut straight to the chase without wasting time on pleasantries. "I heard about the trouble here. Why didn't you call?"

"I thought you were up in the mountains until last

night and figured Mom told you when you called her." Janna glanced at the swing set area by the lodge, where Rylie was in plain sight playing fetch with Maggie. "The DCI was here two days ago, but we might not have any answers for months—possibly even a year."

"So there's no identification? No cause of death?"

Janna shook her head. "Wade thinks it could hurt business here, if rumors start to fly."

"An old skeleton hardly has anything to do with the lodge now." Tessa snorted. "If anything, it'll help get the word out about you reopening the place. How's Mom? Are you two at war yet?"

"I'd hoped things would be different between us now, but they aren't." Janna smiled ruefully. "What makes it harder is that she resents being away from the home place on the ranch, and she's angry at all of us about that. She doesn't understand it's safer for her to be here."

"We expected that."

"And she's forgetful, just as you said. We had a customer arrive for the whole summer, and I had no clue that she'd accepted the reservation. Frankly, I don't think she can be left alone...at least not for more than an afternoon."

Tessa bristled. "She's not a child."

"Her old freedom might have worked back at the ranch, but maybe she's getting a little worse. She refused to come to town with me once. When I got back, she'd opened a can of soup and let it boil dry on the stove. And," Janna added at Tessa's frown, "I'd made her a big lunch just before I left."

"Anyone could make a mistake," Tessa retorted. "I have, though of course you wouldn't. You were always perfect."

Janna took a slow, steadying breath, praying for patience. Years ago, she'd abruptly left the family ranch the night of her high school graduation, after yet another painful confrontation with her mother. Though only two years older than Tessa, Janna had been like a mother figure to her two younger sisters, and they'd surely felt abandoned. She had no illusions about ever being able to bridge the old ravines of hurt and anger without God's healing. But for Claire's sake, at least she had to try.

"I'm just saying that I'm worried about her. We all agreed that Mom would never tolerate a live-in caregiver at the home place. That she'd never, ever agree to residential living. It's fine that she is staying here. I just need to hire an employee, someone who'd be here during the day and who could keep an eye on her—and Riley—if I have to leave for a while." Janna bit at her lower lip. "Unfortunately, I can't afford the salary until I have more paying guests."

"How close is that?"

"Until the entire place is ready? Late fall, maybe—which means I'll miss much of the tourist season this year. But the best four cabins should be ready by early July."

Tessa walked several yards away, then spun back on her heel. "I know of one person who might be willing to come all the way out here. Lauren Young just graduated from high school, and she's had a few rough spots in her life, so she could use a break. I'll get you her number."

"Thanks. I'll give her a call."

The pickup's horn blared, and both sisters turned to see Claire leaning across the seat, her hand at the steering wheel.

Raising a hand in a vague farewell, Tessa jogged back to the truck and climbed behind the wheel. "I'll bring Mom back tomorrow evening," she called out of the window.

Feeling guilty at her sense of temporary freedom, Janna started back to Cabin Five.

Another couple hours of work and the arrival of the appliances would make it completely ready for Michael and his son. One cabin down, nine to go. The soft spring breezes coming over the mountains brought the crisp scents of pines and air so fresh and clean that it almost hurt to breathe. And Rylie, bless her heart, had been entertaining herself all morning while staying close by. Since the discovery of the bones, Janna had barely let the child out of her sight.

"Hey, want to go for a hike with me?" she called out.

Rylie immediately dropped the stick she'd been

throwing for Maggie and came running. "To the waterfall? Can we go that far?"

"Hmm…we'll see." Janna checked her watch. "We
can go for about an hour—unless you want to take a
picnic along. Since Grandma left and the Robertsons
went to town, it's just you and me."

Rylie's eye's danced. "A picnic!"

Fifteen minutes later they were on their way up the
trail, just past the last cabin, with a backpack of food
and Maggie racing around them in circles.

"I don't think we're likely to see any wildlife at
this rate," Janna said dryly when the little dog raced
ahead, barking after yet another butterfly.

"That's good." Rylie shivered and hugged herself,
grinning. "I don't want to meet the bears."

"Bears?"

"Ian says it's scary out here because there's *lots*
of bears, so I shouldn't come out here by myself."

"He does, does he?" Janna mused. "I might need
to have a talk with him about those bears. But he's
right—I don't want you to go on any trails by yourself. You could get lost back here."

Rylie nodded, her eyes big and serious.

"Do you remember what I told you about hug-
ging a tree?"

She thought for a minute. "If I get lost, I shouldn't
keep going."

"Right. Stop where you are. Stay by a big tree, and
don't move until someone finds you." Janna dropped

to one knee, resting her hands on Rylie's shoulders. "It's the people who keep walking and walking who get confused and tired and even more lost. Then it takes a whole lot longer to find them. So hug a tree and stay put."

"I promise, Momma." Rylie ran ahead and caught up with the dog, clearly unconcerned about any dangers that might lurk in the woods.

But even now, with warm, golden sunshine filtering down through the thick canopy of pine boughs and the sweet trilling of birds flitting overhead, Janna felt a sense of foreboding.

Off to the left was the ravine where the skeletal remains had been found. From this angle, she could see down into the mouth of the ravine where the earth had been disturbed, though now all the yellow caution tape had been removed.

On that side of the trail, the investigators had left little sign of their search for evidence. But to the right there were several places where they'd gone digging after something and hadn't taken as much care.

At least it was all over. The remains had been removed. Answers would be found. Life would go on.

Yet even as she firmly recited that litany to herself, an inner voice whispered, *Beware—it's not over yet.*

SIX

After thirteen years away, Janna had expected major changes at the Wolf Creek Community Church, given the growing influx of wealthy Californians into the area.

The exterior gleamed with a new coat of white paint. The parking lot to the south had been asphalted. There appeared to be more headstones marching up the hill to the north, behind the iron grillwork fence dating back to the 1800s.

But the tall, beautiful spire still stretched heavenward, its lacy gingerbread trim intact, and the massive oak doors with mullioned windows were wide-open, as welcoming as ever.

Maybe the people had changed.

But as soon as she and Rylie stepped inside, she knew even that wasn't true. Elderly Mrs. Sawyer still sat at the organ down in front as if she'd never left that very spot, her white head bobbing along with the rhythm of the prelude she was playing.

Pastor Lindsberg was up there, too, seated behind the pulpit. Built like a burly bear-wrestler of old but with a whimsical sense of humor, he'd always been a dynamic and captivating preacher whose deep love of God's Word shone through every sermon he gave.

Even the town's pharmacist and sole funeral director were today's ushers, just as they'd been years ago.

As soon as Janna guided Rylie to a seat in a back pew, she saw a round of subtle shoulder taps, whispers and turning heads—and then familiar faces craning around to search her out: some of Janna's old teachers; Wade, who nodded and smiled; the high school librarian, Mrs. Walker; Harvey, from the feed mill on the edge of town; a few old classmates—though after thirteen years, they looked as different as she probably did, and most of them were a hazy memory at best.

High school had not been a happy time in her life.

"They're *looking* at us, Momma," Rylie whispered, sliding down in her seat. "How come?"

Janna gave her a reassuring pat, then curled a hand around Rylie's. "Because I grew up here, and it's been a long time since I left. In a town this small, people notice."

Especially when you leave in the dark of night and never come back.

When heads started turning toward the other side of the church, she glanced over to the right and found Ian and Michael seated at the back. Ian was slouched, his head hung low and the tips of his ears red—a sure sign he was all too aware of the attention.

Michael, movie-star handsome in a perfectly cut suede blazer and khakis, sat next to him. He smiled at someone in front of him who had turned around, his dimples deepening and his teeth flashing white against his tan.

He glanced over, and Janna felt her pulse pick up when their gazes collided, held, then veered away. Did he feel it, too—that subtle sense of awareness, even from across the room?

From the corner of her eye, she saw him shift in his seat and whisper something to Ian, then they both looked up at the beautiful old stained-glass window above the altar.

Easily over a hundred years old by now, its intricate, richly colored depiction of Jesus and his flock had entranced her from the first moment she'd ever walked into this church as a shy and awkward girl of ten, on the arm of her great-Aunt Sarah.

Claire had rarely found the time for Sunday-morning trips to church, but when Aunt Sarah moved back from New York, she'd promptly begun rounding up the McAllister girls every Sunday without fail.

Sarah had brought them to faith and had provided the kind of gentle nurturing that none of them had experienced at home. She was at her heavenly peace now, resting beneath a modest headstone on the hill outside, and when she died, she'd taken a big piece of Janna's heart with her.

Rylie nudged her. "Momma, are you sad?"

"Just remembering, sweetheart. Remembering some dear old friends."

Mrs. Sawyer launched into the first bars of "How Great Thou Art" and with just the first notes, Janna felt a sense of peace and comfort surround her that lasted through the rest of the service. The passages from John 14, read during the lesson and echoed in the sermon topic, kept playing through her thoughts. "…Peace I leave with you; my peace I give to you. I do not give to you as the world gives. Do not let your hearts be troubled and do not be afraid."

Perfect words, given at a perfect time…which happened so often when she listed to a sermon or turned to read passages from her Bible.

After the final hymn, Janna curved an arm around Rylie's shoulder and moved down the aisle with the crowd to shake the pastor's hand at the door.

"Good to see you," he boomed. "It's been a long, long time. And who's this young lady?"

Rylie ducked her head and hung back, then shyly extended her hand. He enveloped her hand between his own massive paws. "Pretty as a picture—just like your mom. Y'all come back next week, okay?"

Janna grinned, enjoying the folksy Texas accent he'd retained despite moving north decades earlier. "We'll definitely do that."

"Maybe you can even get your momma and Tessa to come along." He winked at her. "There's plenty of room."

But probably not enough room in Claire's stubborn heart…and after a traumatic incident in Tessa's life during her early twenties, she'd fallen away as well. "I'll pray about it," Janna said.

"Me, too." They chatted for another minute, and when the pastor turned to greet some others, a trio of women came to stand in front of Janna, their smiles genuine but uncertainty flickering in their eyes.

Janna blinked, taking in familiar features blurred by added weight and the passage of time. Still…

"Betsy? Maria? And—oh, my word. *Ivy?*" She took a deep breath and hugged each of her old classmates in turn. As a ranch girl, she'd had an hour bus ride each way and had been too isolated to develop strong bonds with the town girls, but these three had been the closest friends she'd had, even if their friendship had been limited to the hours during school itself. "It's been such a long time!"

"You disappeared the day of graduation," Maria whispered. "We were *worried*. Your mom was always sooo mean to you, and—"

"Maria!" Frowning, Betsy tilted her head toward the churchgoers who might be within hearing distance.

"Well, it's true," Maria countered. "We called the ranch, but your mom never returned our calls and the housekeeper wouldn't—or couldn't—say where you'd gone." Casting a quick glance at Rylie, who had wandered over to stand with Ian, she lowered her voice even further. "Your sisters cried when we asked them and said you'd gone away to school but they didn't know where. We figured something *awful* happened to you."

It had. That terrible last fight with her mother, after years of friction, had been the last straw. Even now, remembering the fear and uncertainty of driving off into the night in one of the ranch trucks, not knowing if Aunt Sarah would take her in, had the power to twist Janna's stomach into a painful knot.

But it touched her deeply that these old school friends had cared enough to try to find her, because with all the bitterness she'd felt, she'd totally cut her ties back home. "I…did go straight to college. I was already registered at Wyoming U for the fall, so my aunt helped me register early for summer school and helped me move."

Though if it hadn't been for a full-ride scholarship, Janna would've been back to square one, because Claire never would've paid college fees for a daughter she'd essentially disowned.

For years she'd even refused to speak to Janna on the phone.

"We heard more later on," Ivy said. "So we knew you were okay. But then we were soon off to college, too, and we all lost track of each other for a while." She smiled. "Now I'm a rancher's wife—I married

Marty, one of the Jacobson boys. Maria works at her father's bank, and Betsy's managing her dad's cow-calf operation. Funny, isn't it? That we all ended up back here?"

"Funny," Janna echoed faintly. For years, she'd managed to lock away most of the troubling memories from her teen years and concentrate on just the happier times, but now everything came flooding back. "I…I hope we'll have a chance to visit sometime soon."

Betsy leaned forward for a quick hug. "Absolutely."

Michael moved to her side when the trio of women walked away. "Best friends?"

"Once upon a time, though I haven't seen them since high school. Friends," she added quietly after a moment's thought, "whose families have lived in the area for generations. I wonder—do you suppose any of their older relatives might remember talk about someone who went missing in the area, long ago?"

Michael's gaze sharpened. "I've had my officers talking to people in the area, but they've come up dry so far. Any reason why these people would be of interest?"

"Maria's family has owned the local bank for generations. Maybe one of them might remember someone in trouble and desperate. Betsy's in-laws have owned land bordering my mother's place to the east for just as long. And Ivy—" Janna hesitated. "Well, her dad is a straight-up guy, but if you're the law around here for long, you're sure to run into her uncles, and it won't just be to say 'hello.' Seems like someone in one of these families might know something, if anyone would."

Michael glanced at Ian and tipped his head toward their truck, then threaded his arm through the crook of Janna's elbow. "Can I walk you ladies to your car?"

She nodded, but waited until they'd reached her Snow Canyon Ranch pickup and Rylie had climbed in before continuing her thought. "I've tried to talk to my mother about the…situation…out at the lodge."

The laugh lines at the corners of Michael's eyes deepened. "I hope you've had better luck than I have."

"Hardly. Each time, she brushes me off and then gets irritable if I persist. I got the same sort of reaction from Fred at the grocery store."

"Fred?"

"The owner. He's pushing seventy, but he stopped me one day to ask about the rumors. I told him I didn't know anything, then asked him some questions about the past. He suddenly got busy and had no time to answer. It made me think about a magazine article I once read. What if this is one of those situations where everyone knows the truth, but no one dares reveal it?"

"Well," Janna said, dusting off her hands. "What do you think? Will your dad be pleased?"

For a place without cable, TV reception or a hot

tub, it was okay. But she looked so happy about the curtains and bright-red woven rugs in Cabin Five that Ian dredged up a half grin. "It's fine."

"I don't want to be intrusive and handle any of your dad's things when he isn't here. But I'd be happy to help you guys move this evening when he comes home." She paused and looked around. "If you'd like to bring your own luggage up now, we could do that."

Ian started to say no, then reconsidered. The cabin was nice and private. Out of sight of the main lodge, where that grumpy old lady always seemed to be giving him dirty looks—even when he wasn't in her way. How Janna had ended up nice with a mother like that one was—

The thought hit him like a sucker punch to the stomach. As always, whenever he felt blindsided by a word or photo or a sudden memory, his breath caught, his eyes started to burn, and he wanted to turn around and drive a fist into the wall.

It was so unfair. So cruel and overwhelming and still so unbelievable. All the more, because a nasty woman like Claire McAllister had stuck around to old age, while his own mom…

He blinked. Wanted to run. Hide—anything, to get away from the sympathy in Janna's eyes and the rush of humiliation that clogged his throat. He didn't cry. *Ever.* But though he wanted to keep her from seeing his tears, he couldn't seem to make his feet move.

She stepped closer and rested her hands on his

shoulders. Warmth seemed to flow through him and settle around his aching heart at her touch. "Your father told me about the accident, Ian. There just aren't enough words to express how sorry I am that you've had to go through this."

He bowed his head, unable to speak.

"I know you're a big guy, and you barely know me—but if you ever need to talk, I'm here."

Part of him wanted that more than anything. Another part rebelled, angry and defiant at the offer of sympathy from yet another person who could never understand how gut-wrenching his grief and guilt were.

There'd already been way too many shallow condolences. People who'd said terrible things like, "Maybe it was meant to be" when the only thing he wanted was to have Mom back with him. Alive and laughing and carefree.

Like she'd been before her own son had managed to kill her.

He leaned into Janna's touch for a moment, then jerked away and fled to the door without looking back. He knew that if he stayed any longer, he might start crying like a baby. And what was the use of that?

Outside, Rylie looked up from petting her dog and smiled at him. "It's a nice cabin, isn't it? I helped make the beds, and—"

He rushed past her, ignoring a sharp twinge in his knee. He hesitated, then turned up the lane leading to the trails beyond the last cabin. He needed space and solitude and a place where he could scream if he wanted to, and no one would hear.

"Ian! Wait!" Rylie's voice followed him, but he didn't look back…not until he'd gone way past the last cabin and reached the place where the trail split into three directions. He saw her from a distance, doggedly starting up the long, rock-strewn hill.

Great.

He wavered, then took the trail to the right—just a faint track leading through a dense thicket, and one he'd never explored. No one would think to follow him here.

Rylie would surely give up—she always turned back. And this was one time when he really wanted to be alone.

After dealing with a multicar accident, a domestic disturbance and a vandalism report during the afternoon—the last of which had been just a few miles from town—Michael sighed with relief when he pulled in at Snow Canyon Lodge at four o'clock.

Finding this place had been an answer to his prayers. It was beyond beautiful, in the shadows of rugged mountain peaks that rose like snow-frosted sentinels to the west. It offered solitude, and more opportunity for trying to bond with Ian. The evening meals had been exceptional. And Janna…

She truly was a lovely woman; caring and so determined to succeed, with a refreshing sense of humor and a calm, down-to-earth approach despite what must have been a difficult life.

He found himself looking forward to the end of each day, so he could seek her out for conversation. He felt an inexplicable level of disappointment if he ended up working late and missed those visits. She was—

Running straight for him, her face pale.

He stepped out of the patrol car and caught her gently by the upper arms a split second before she would've barreled right into his chest.

"She's gone—Rylie's gone!"

"Since when?" He held her at arm's length. "What happened?"

"I—was just finishing up your cabin and talking to Ian. He got a little emotional—I'm not sure why—and he stormed out. I think he went off on a hike for a while to cool off. Rylie was playing with Maggie in the yard." Janna drew in a shuddering breath. "But after I went up to the lodge to make a late lunch, I called and called and looked everywhere. Rylie left Maggie behind, and now it's been several hours. She's *never* stayed away this long. And why would she leave her dog?"

"Did you ask Ian if he'd seen her?"

"He showed up maybe a half hour after I started looking, but said he didn't have any idea where she was. He and I have been searching for her ever since."

"Where is he now?"

"I…I don't know. He…he came back to me and asked if she'd turned up, then disappeared. I was just going to call you."

"So we might have two kids lost."

She blanched.

"Tell me exactly where you've looked for her."

Janna raised a trembling hand and pointed toward the long lane to the highway. "I went down there, calling her name, though she knows she'd not supposed to leave the resort area. I've been up the trails to east and south, and I've checked all the cabins. Now all I can think about is the night I saw someone out in the woods with a flashlight. He seemed to realize that he'd been spotted, because he hurried away. What if he grabbed my daughter?"

"Has she ever gone off by herself before? Does she have any secret forts? Places she loves to hide?"

"I know she likes following Ian when he goes for his little hikes, but he said she wasn't with him today. He…seemed pretty upset about it."

Upset…or guilty? Michael set his jaw. "Did he say which way he went?"

"The trails past Cabin Ten. But I've already been up there, too. She wasn't at the waterfall, and that's the only place she's ever been in that direction." Janna's voice caught, and she trembled within Michael's gentle grasp. "Unless…the water could be so deep there. What if she went wading and hit a drop off?"

The thought had crossed his mind, too, though

there'd be no hope of rescue by now if that were the case. "I doubt she'd put more than a toe in that water—those mountain streams are ice cold this time of year."

Some of the tension in Janna's body seemed to ease. "You're right. Of course you are."

"What about your mother?"

"I told her to stay in the house and call my cell phone if Rylie showed up." Janna gave him a wobbly smile. "For once, I think she actually listened to me."

Michael released her, pivoted toward his car and reached inside to grab the mike.

He turned back to her a minute later. "The other two officers are at least an hour away, and dispatch is calling in the county search-and-rescue team. They've got a dog handler who's had a lot of success with lost hikers in the mountains, so I'd guess we'll have your daughter and Ian back in no time flat." He scanned the lodge grounds slowly, considering the possibilities. *Please, Lord, send me in the right direction—and please, please keep both children safe from harm.*

There were still three hours or so before nightfall, but by the time the other officers or the search team showed up, there'd be little daylight left. Nightfall, even in June, meant temps in the forties at this altitude.

A cold night for a child dressed for the warmth of a sunny afternoon.

A terrifying experience for a child alone…who could wander over a steep cliff and fall to her death or be stalked by predators that wouldn't hesitate to size up a defenseless child as easy prey.

The one direction that seemed right was straight west toward the mountains, where there were pretty trails and waterfalls, according to Ian. "I want you to stay here," he said over his shoulder.

"But—"

"No." He turned back to her. "When the others arrive, you need to give them a piece of Rylie's clothing—and get something of Ian's, too. You can point out where you've been looking and show them where I've gone. I need you here, Janna."

She gave him a jerky nod, her face white.

He wanted to go back and enfold her in a long and reassuring embrace, and promise her that everything would be okay.

But he'd learned from long experience that wasted seconds could lead to heartbreak, and there just wasn't time.

With another prayer on his lips, he took off at a run.

SEVEN

Michael kept a steady pace past the cabins and the ravine where the bones had been discovered.

The trail narrowed, winding up through steep, rocky outcroppings and thick stands of pines, where dirty patches of snow still lingered in the deepest shadows. Every few yards he paused to shout Ian's and Rylie's names.

Halfway up he had to stop and rest, breathless from the altitude and his fast pace; not yet adapted to the thinner air at over six thousand feet. It was colder up here, too—noticeably different from the sunny meadow where the lodge stood.

Was Rylie curled up in some nearly invisible place, shivering? Hurt and in shock? There were emergency supplies in the backpack he'd grabbed out of his patrol car, but would they be enough to handle whatever he found? Had Ian come up here after her, only to take a completely different turn?

Michael pulled out his cell phone to check its

range. A single reception bar flickered on the screen, which meant that even if Rylie and Ian had already turned up at the cabins, he might not be able to receive that message.

Still, an inner voice drove him on, and a sixth sense told him that they hadn't turned up safe and sound. Not yet.

Another hundred yards brought him to the fork where the main trail wound off to the left, and a faint deer trail veered to the right. He bent low, searching for a sign that anyone had headed a certain way. The pebbles and patches of exposed granite held no trace of passersby.

Shouting Ian's name, he moved ten, fifteen feet in each direction, his hopes fading. Then he went back and checked again.

Where did the boy go when he got up this far? And had Rylie followed him?

Up to the right, Michael pulled back a clump of underbrush crowding over the trail. Here, in a damp patch of earth, he could make out the faint crescent of a heel print—fresh enough that the rim hadn't yet dried and crumbled into the impression. *Thank you, Lord, for your many mercies.*

He took off at a fast jog now, keeping a close eye on the ground where the trail traversed long stretches of granite. Backtracking, where the trail faded out into one dead end after another.

A branch cracked up the trail. Then another. Pebbles rolled down a rocky incline. He stilled, listening. A hiker? A bear? The kids?

Hope surged through him as he pulled a heavy traffic whistle from his pocket and delivered two sharp blasts. If Ian was ahead, had he thought to bring his own, as he'd been told?

No answering whistle sounded—but when Michael reached the next bend, Ian's voice echoed out over the terrain. "Dad? Dad! Is that you?"

Then Ian appeared, his face scratched and bleeding. Limping heavily, he struggled over the rocky, uneven path…with Rylie sobbing in his arms.

Given the downward slope and the effect of gravity, it should have been a faster trip back, but loose gravel, underbrush and the old injury in Ian's knee made the descent nearly as slow as the trip up… though the relief in Michael's heart overflowed every step of the way. *Thank you, dear Lord, for your protection of these children.*

Halfway down, he'd been able to find enough cell phone reception to call off the search-and-rescue team and let Janna know that all was well.

Rylie, her arms looped around Michael's neck, looked up at him with worried eyes. "Is my mom mad?"

"Terribly worried. And terribly scared about what might've happened to you. The rest, you'll have to ask her." Michael nodded down the trail. "There she is. See her, past those rocks?"

Tears welled up in Rylie's eyes. "I didn't mean to cause any trouble. I was only following Ian, because he looked so sad."

A few yards behind them, Ian muttered something under his breath.

"Did he see you following him?"

"I…" her eyes grew troubled. "I don't know. I couldn't catch up, and then I got lost. It's my fault, honest. Please don't be mad at him."

Janna made it up the trail to meet them within minutes. The radiant joy in her face transformed her from lovely to breathtaking, her cheeks flushed and eyes sparkling as she cradled Rylie's face in her hands and brushed a kiss against the child's forehead. "Oh, Rylie—I was so worried about you."

Michael gently put Rylie down on a boulder so Janna could envelop her in a hug, then check her over from head to foot. She cradled Rylie's bandaged ankle gently in both hands. "Just the ankle, sweetheart? Is that all that hurts?"

Rylie winced at her mother's light touch, then held out her palm, which Michael had also bandaged. "And this, from when I fell."

"Why ever did you come clear up here?"

The child shot a furtive, guilty look toward Ian, then dropped her gaze.

"You know the rules. We talked about them the very first day here, and a dozen times since then. Right?"

Rylie nodded, her lower lip trembling.

"Why should you never go up here alone?"

Rylie gave her mother a stricken look, then fixed her gaze on her hands. "Bears. Mountain lions. Maybe wolves sometimes."

"Right. A child alone could seem like easy prey. We'll get you into town and have a doctor take a look at your ankle to make sure you don't have a fracture. But fracture or sprain, you'll be in the house for a while…and after that, we'll talk about this again." She turned to Ian and smiled. "And this time I do get to give you a hug."

She embraced him warmly, then stood back and held his hands with both of her own. "I can't thank you enough for finding Rylie. With that injured ankle she never could've made it back alone. We might not have found her for hours, maybe days. You probably saved her life."

He blushed a furious red that reached his cheekbones and the tips of his ears.

"What about you—can you make it home all right? This was a hard hike for all of us," she added tactfully.

Ian nodded, fumbling for the long branch he'd picked up along the way to use as a walking stick. He carefully pushed himself back to his feet and started making his way down the trail.

"He and I have will have a conversation when we get back," Michael said in a low voice. "I think he needs to accept some responsibility for this situation."

"But he found her. He brought her back—and

honestly, right now that's all that matters to me. I'll always be grateful for that."

"Let's get you home, young lady." Michael lifted Rylie into his arms and started down the trail after Ian, with Janna right behind him. "It'll be dusk soon, and we can all talk about it later."

By the time they neared the ravine, the lengthening shadows had cast the surrounding forest in near darkness.

Michael shifted Rylie's weight in his arms. "Almost home, sugar. I'll bet you'll be glad to put your foot up on a pillow and rest after this."

"Wait." Janna's voice came from a few yards back. "That's really odd—unless it's just my imagination."

He turned and found her staring off the side of the trail, pointing to several low clumps of underbrush. "What is?"

"Last Thursday, I saw several places over there—you know, where the DCI dug for evidence." She leaned forward and peered into the gloom. "I thought they were done, didn't you? Now it looks like they've been back."

He retraced his steps and followed the direction of her hand. "The DCI didn't spend any time over there, Janna. I was with them the entire day. They excavated the burial site and spent considerable time in the ravine. They wouldn't come back, much less research such a distant site, without contacting me first. They come by invitation, not as an independent agency."

"But look—see there, by those trees? There were several piles of fresh dirt last week—now I'm almost certain there are more." She visibly shivered. "You don't think…"

He searched around for a place for Rylie to sit, then put her down on a log. "You two stay here and I'll go take a look."

Without a trail, it took several minutes to make his way through the low-lying brush, downed trees and twisted vines.

Sure enough—there were five haphazard holes here, not more than fifteen feet apart. Perhaps four feet square, they'd been partially refilled with loose dirt and leaves, with mounds of loose branches tossed on top. To shield them from view?

Had they been dug to bury something—or to search for something else?

Michael hunkered down and sifted the loose soil through his fingers, then scanned the area. McAllister land stretched at least a mile toward the closest boundary. The only vehicle access into the area was the long, narrow road leading to the lodge—which meant a high risk of being noticed.

If someone wanted to hide something, surely they wouldn't go to this much trouble and still be so close to an inhabited set of buildings. It made no sense.

But if someone was *looking* for something, that opened up a new realm of possibilities. What sort of determination—or desperation—could drive a person to dig in this rocky, hard-packed terrain? With the scant annual rainfall in the area, a pickax was probably required to make any progress at all.

As soon as the sun rose tomorrow, Michael would be back, and he would be hunting for answers.

Startled by a knock on her door, Claire leaned forward in her chair and peered over her shoulder, her June copy of the *Western Rancher* open on her lap.

The words had run together, spiraling across the page in dizzying patterns since she'd sat down an hour ago, and irritation welled up in her throat at the interruption.

"Mom, are you in there? Are you okay?"

Janna. *Again.* Claire slammed her magazine shut. It was always something. That obnoxious teenage boy thundering down the stairs and slamming doors. Rylie, who'd foolishly gotten herself lost yesterday and acted like a scared rabbit half the time.

Or Janna—who had to be mighty proud of her little power trip here at the lodge. Always interfering. Prying. Watching. As if Claire had ever needed help from anyone in her entire life.

"I'm busy," Claire barked, stubbornly sitting back in her chair.

The door squealed open anyway, and Janna walked right on in to stand in front of Claire. "I couldn't hear you answer. Are you all right?"

Claire's anger escalated to rage, swift and hot.

"Why wouldn't I be? Go…do whatever it is you're doing around here, and leave me in peace."

As usual, Janna didn't listen. Instead, her eyebrows drew together and she searched Claire's face. "I just came in from working on one of the cabins to start lunch. The bathtub was overflowing, Mom. There's even water in the hall."

"The tub?" Claire stared blankly at her, her anger dissipating in a swirl of anxiety and confusion. "I don't know what you're talking about."

Janna hunkered down in front of Claire's chair at eye level, as if talking to a child. "I've been outside. Rylie is out in the lobby watching TV, with her foot propped on pillows," she said with a smile. "No one else was in the lodge. Maybe you started running a bath and just got distracted? That can happen to anyone."

"I certainly didn't do it," Claire snapped, angered at the gentle compassion in Janna's eyes. "It had to be that fool child of yours."

Janna sighed and rocked back on her heels. "It couldn't have been, but it doesn't matter. I've mopped up everything, so you can take your bath now, if you'd like."

"I never take a bath this time of day." Claire sniffed. "If I were you, I'd be mighty careful about believing what that Rylie says."

At a tiny, horrified gasp, Claire glanced sharply toward the door and saw Rylie standing there on her crutches, her face white and eyes brimming with sudden tears. Eavesdropping, no doubt.

Janna was at the girl's side in an instant. Wrapping her in a hug. Coddling her. Then she looked over her shoulder at Claire, sparks flashing in her eyes. "Rylie is an honest and loving little girl," Janna said evenly. "And I believe what she says. Let's just drop this, okay?"

Claire snorted.

"Honey, go on back to your room for a minute, okay?" Janna brushed a kiss against Rylie's forehead and helped her maneuver the crutches so she could head down the hall. "Grandma and I need to talk for a minute."

Janna watched her make her way down the hall, then turned back to Claire, her arms folded across her chest. "I'm glad we're living here together, so you two can get to know each other better. Your granddaughter is the sweetest little girl you could imagine."

Claire impatiently slapped her magazine against her lap and opened it to a random page.

Janna ignored the obvious dismissal and pulled a chair up to face her. "Look, I know we have a tough history. But let's keep that between the two of us, okay? Rylie doesn't deserve your anger."

"Tough history?" Incredulous, Claire stared at her. "I'm not the one who never pitched in around here."

"I tried, Mom. You just never thought I did anything well enough." She took a steadying breath. "Not like Tessa—she was always so much better at ranch work."

"And I'm not the one who cut out in the middle of the night and never looked back."

"We were always at odds, you and me." Janna smiled sadly. "I'm hoping that will change. In the meantime, I need you to be a little nicer to Rylie. Her other grandma—"

"I don't have to listen to this." Claire threw her magazine across the room and launched to her feet. Brushing past Janna, she strode down the hall to the private back entrance, automatically grabbing for a set of keys as she shoved the screen door open and stalked outside.

But it wasn't possible for Claire to outrun the nagging voice in her head. Not if she walked the trails for hours, not if she got behind the wheel and drove ninety down the endless Wyoming highways. *Just like your brother. Just like your brother.*

Her brother, Gray, had succumbed to Alzheimer's long before he died last year, but there was no way she'd let that happen to her. He'd been weak. He didn't have the resolve to look adversity in the eye and dare anyone—or anything—to stand in his way.

She'd never give in.

Still, guilt nipped at the edge of her conscience. Had she turned on that water, then totally forgotten about it? And what about the other times, when her mind went completely blank?

At the edge of the porch she looked down at the hard, cold objects in her hand, panic turning her palms damp and sending her heart tripping into overdrive.

A wisp of a thought drifted through her brain. Dissipated. Then finally took form.

Keys. I was going someplace...but where?

Two useless husbands who'd died young, leaving her with a family to raise on her own and a struggling ranch had taught her harsh lessons. She'd learned long ago that believing in anyone except herself was a waste of time.

Raw fear hit her with the force of a stallion's kick to her stomach, and from some forgotten recess of her memory, bits and pieces of a rusty prayer filtered to the surface, though most of the words were too elusive to catch.

Now a new litany began to run through her head. *Please, God...please...help me....*

EIGHT

Claire had been gone for hours, Janna realized.

She'd been a capable driver all her life. Too fast, too impatient, but she'd negotiated the local mountain roads with the absolute focus of a race driver, and she'd never had an accident. She'd also spent her entire life in this area.

But now she was forgetful. A tad confused at times. And despite her grudging promise, she'd driven off without Tessa or Janna along. So where on earth was she?

A dozen old headlines marched through Janna's thoughts—the ones about addled grandfathers leaving home for milk and ending up in Orlando or Denver, and elderly women ending up at a mission in some distant city, with no memory of their own names or how they'd gotten there.

Claire certainly wasn't at that stage yet...or was she?

Worry knotted Janna's stomach as she hauled

crumbling, mildewed furniture out of Cabin One. She ran up to the lodge to ask Rylie if anyone had called, then hurried back again to add more things to the growing pile of refuse in front of the cabin, though every few minutes she listened for the sound of an old pickup rattling up the lane. *Mom is probably fine…just running some errands. Talking to someone she saw in town. She's made that trip a million times.*

It was a forty-mile drive on winding, two-lane asphalt, and the round-trip itself took a couple hours; errands and chitchat with neighbors could add another hour or more.

But Claire wasn't a talker.

What could possibly take this long in a town of twelve hundred people? Unless she'd had a doctor or dental appointment that she hadn't bothered to mention…or had run out of gas along the way.

At two in the afternoon, Janna called the grocery store in town to casually ask if Claire had been there yet, as "there were some extra groceries she needed to pick up." After that, Janna had called the feed store, gas station and even a park ranger to the north, all on the pretext of needing to give Claire a message, in an effort to save her mother's fierce pride.

No one had seen her.

At three Janna gave up trying to scrub away decades of dirt in Cabin One and called Michael's cell phone. He didn't answer, but she left a message asking him to keep an eye out for Claire's truck. Then she went back to the lodge, where Rylie was happily ensconced on a cushy leather chair by the massive stone fireplace in the lodge, watching a Disney movie. Her fractured right ankle was in a cast and propped up on a matching ottoman.

"We need to go for a ride, honey. I'm a little worried about your grandma being gone so long."

Rylie's cheerful smile faded. "I don't want to go. My ankle hurts."

"I know, but I can't just leave you here." Smiling, Janna jingled her keys. "We could get a sundae at the drugstore."

Rylie's mouth formed a mutinous pout. "What about Ian? Maybe he could stay with me."

"I'm not sure he'd want to babysit, sweetie. He's here as a paying guest." And, given the boy's bristly attitude at times, Janna wasn't sure she'd even want to ask.

Yet another reason Janna was thankful that Tessa's friend Lauren was coming for an interview tomorrow morning. Having an extra adult at the lodge—even if just part-time—would be a blessing in many ways.

After helping Rylie maneuver her cast and crutches into their car, Janna started down the long ranch road. "Keep an eye out for Grandma, okay?"

Rylie slouched lower in her seat. "Why doesn't she like me?"

Old emotions welled up in Janna's throat as bits of her own childhood came back to her. The hurt. The anger. The feeling of being unlovable, and of never measuring up.

It took her a while to find the right words.

"Your grandmother is an amazing woman, honey. She had to be tough and smart to run a ranch and raise her children alone. So, she…she never really had time to be a chocolate-chip-cookies-and-warm-hugs kind of mom. I guess that's still her way."

Though even as Janna defended her, an old, small voice whispered that things could have been different. Should have been better. If Claire had been able to love her daughters more, maybe all three of them would be happier now.

From the hurt expression in her eyes, Rylie clearly wasn't convinced. "She mostly just yells as me. She's always mad."

"Maybe she's more impatient because she's old, and a little scared because she can't remember very well. But I know that deep inside she loves you very much. Maybe we should pray extra hard for her."

"So she'll be nice?"

Janna hid a smile. "To help her feel better. And to help her heart so she won't be so unhappy."

There was no sign of the ranch pickup along the lane or on the curving highway leading down into Wolf Creek. Janna talked with clerks in the grocery store, the feed store, the drugstore and the lone gas station on the edge of town—all to no avail. No one even remembered seeing a Snow Canyon Ranch pickup in town today.

And Tessa was out of reception range, high up in the mountains on another pack trip, according to the ranch hand who'd answered the phone in the barn at the home place. He hadn't seen Claire, either. *Where on earth could she be?*

Janna pulled to the side of the highway outside of town, her fears rising. She took a slow, calming breath and started another silent prayer.

Her cell phone jangled.

Rylie looked up from her hot-fudge sundae. "Maybe that's Grandma, and she's already home!"

But it wasn't Claire's voice on the other end of the line. It was Michael's. "I got a call just minutes ago," he said. "A truck driver on County 63 saw an elderly woman walking on the highway by the Wolf Creek Bridge and was concerned enough to report it. His description of her sounds like your mother, and she…told him to mind his own business when he offered her a ride. I'm on my way over there now."

Thank you, Lord. "I'll meet you there—ten minutes or less."

Janna did a quick three-point turn and headed back into town to the main intersection, then turned west on County 63. A couple miles out she came upon Michael's white patrol car parked at the side of the road. He was leaning against the hood, one booted foot crossed casually over the other and his arms folded.

And sure enough, there was Claire—her face red with anger, her hands jammed on her bony hips.

The ranch truck wasn't in sight.

"Wow," Rylie breathed, leaning forward in her seat to peer out the front window. "I've never seen her that mad!"

"Stay in the car, sweetie," Janna said, pulling to a stop in a shady spot behind the cruiser. She opened all of the electric windows. "This shouldn't take long."

Michael turned and smiled at Janna as she approached. "Your mother had some car trouble," he said. "But she's fine."

He radiated such an air of calm, quiet strength that Janna felt her tension ease.

Claire snorted. "*Car trouble?* Having two flat tires in front is not happenstance. Someone vandalized my truck."

Michael didn't appear convinced. "It's…possible though she did do a U-turn up the road a ways and might have run over some scrap metal."

Claire glared at him. "I didn't. It was *vandals*."

Michael tipped his head in agreement, though Janna guessed he was trying to tactfully defuse the situation. "You mother changed one of the tires, but didn't have a second spare. She was hiking back to town."

"Someone hoped I'd lose control and die," Claire added darkly. "This was no accident."

Michael picked up a clipboard lying on the hood of his car. "One of the rims was damaged when she veered off the road, Janna. I called the garage in town, and they'll be out shortly with a new tire and rim."

Janna drew a sharp breath, thinking about how serious this could've been.

"I was just asking if she'd had words with someone in town," Michael added. "Or knew of anyone else who might be angry at her. Or if she remembered running over anything."

"Of course not," Claire said coldly, her chin lifted at an imperious angle.

"Where have you been all this time?" Janna searched her mother's sunburned face. "I've been worried, Mom."

Claire's eyes narrowed. "I went to check on my herd of Charolais, then stopped at the Lost Horse Café for coffee. I'm certainly not a child. I can go where I please."

The café was a new one in town since Janna's childhood, and she hadn't thought to call there. The explanation sounded logical, except… "Where were you headed next?"

"Home, of course," Claire snapped.

Yet after a lifetime of living in this county, she'd taken the wrong highway out of town.

Between the possible vandalism of her truck and the dangers that could arise from Claire's confusion, things at Snow Canyon Lodge had just taken a turn for the worse.

Janna shielded her eyes against the rays of late-afternoon sunshine angling through the pines and watched Ian and Michael come down the lane from Cabin Five.

Since his long hike searching for Rylie, Ian had been limping noticeably more, and he'd seemed even more subdued than usual.

Even so, the two of them had insisted on handling the move to their cabin alone. After the second trip with their pickup, they'd stayed up there—unpacking, probably, and settling in.

"So, what do you think?" she called out. "Cozy enough?"

"Great." Michael stopped at the bottom of the porch steps and looked up at her, his eyes somber. "We have a proposition for you. Ian?"

The boy pulled to an ungainly stop next to him, his eyes fixed on the ground. The top curve of his ears turned pink. "I…we want to help you out. Because… it was sorta my fault that Rylie got lost."

His voice had dropped to an almost indistinguishable mumble by the time he apologized, but Janna knew how much that admission had cost him. She came down the steps, wishing she dared hug him but not sure he would accept it.

The awkward machismo of teenage boys was out of her realm, and this one was emotionally wounded, to boot.

"Rylie shouldn't have followed you, and I'm just thankful that you could help find her, Ian. Without you, we still might be looking." She briefly clasped one of his hands. "I think we're square, don't you?"

"We, uh, figured we could maybe help fix up some of your cabins." Ian toed at a tuft of wiry grass. "Since you need more time to take care of Rylie now."

"I see." Janna hid a smile at the boy's obvious reluctance and nearly declined, then realized this was a lesson his father wanted to teach. "That's very thoughtful."

"We talked it over," Michael said. "Ian and I could help with some carpentry projects in the evenings, when I get home from work."

Ian met his dad's gaze, and when Michael nodded, the boy turned and headed back toward their cabin.

"But you're paying guests here. Surely you'd like to just kick back and relax after work." She waved a hand toward the cabins that marched up the hill like tired old soldiers, all in need of significant rehab. "Believe me, this isn't much fun."

Michael shrugged. "Consider it a favor. Ian and I haven't exactly had the best relationship, and a little manly bonding over a hammer and pliers could be a good thing."

"Well…maybe just for a few evenings. No further obligations, in case Ian loathes that sort of bonding." She grinned. "Deal?"

"Deal." He thrust out a hand.

She accepted his warm, firm handshake and felt her heart skip.

He was a good man, solid and true, and she found herself wishing that their circumstances were different. What would it be like to love a man like him? A man who would be a steadfast husband and a good father to a child in all the ways that really counted?

Even after she withdrew her hand, she felt the reassuring warmth of Michael's touch. "I...didn't want to say anything earlier, with Ian or Rylie around, but thanks for your help with my mother this afternoon. I know she can be a little testy."

"Frankly, I think she was scared, finding herself heading in the wrong direction, then having those flat tires."

"A little frightened, but also still her obstinate self. About the flats—I don't imagine they were a coincidence."

"I doubt it. The guys at the garage said they found identical nails in those tires. I asked a few questions at the café, but no one saw anyone lurking around her truck. Your mom parked at the side of the building, though, so someone could've crept up without being seen. Or, it could've happened at your place. Nails can cause a slow leak."

"But why would anyone do that? An old grudge against her, maybe? Surely this wasn't just a random teenage prank."

"Last week you told me about a guy who threatened you when you were in town. Have you seen him again?"

She shivered. "Nope. I tried describing him to the clerks in the grocery and drugstore, but he just sounded like a lot of other cowboys to them."

"If you see him, call me." Michael set his jaw, and his voice dropped a good ten degrees. "If there's anyone else nearby, see if they can identify him, but don't approach him."

Janna nodded. "What about the cold murder case you've been checking—any luck?"

"It's strange." Michael's brow furrowed. "This is a small town, a sparsely populated county. Missing persons and suspicions of murder should stir up a lot of speculation, yet I haven't found a single pertinent article in the local newspaper archives. Nothing in the files at the sheriff's office that fits the bill, either."

Janna sighed. "So that's it, then?"

"We might not have that DCI report for many months. Back ten, twenty years ago, few small jurisdictions were computerized, and the most rural ones might never get all of their old records logged in." He rubbed his jaw. "So the DCI doesn't have records of every last missing person—and might not be able to identify the remains found on your property."

"But…"

"I still have a hunch we're going to find something. Why else would someone be digging on your property? I went out early this morning and took another look. It's clear that someone tried to camouflage their handiwork—and that it wasn't done long ago, either. The needles on those pine branches were still soft."

"Probably that guy I saw slipping through the trees with a flashlight." Janna took a shaky breath. "And in the meantime, you and I both have children at the lodge and cabins—less than a hundred yards away."

"I'm going to alternate with one of my officers for the next week or so and maintain surveillance of that area. In the meantime I want Ian and Rylie staying close to home."

"Agreed," Janna said fervently.

It was a good plan. Far more than she would've expected, given the situation and the limited manpower in the sheriff's department.

But surveillance couldn't last forever. The stranger might stay clear until he knew no one was watching… and he might have all the time in the world to wait.

So how was she going to keep her family and guests safe?

NINE

"Surely you don't want to spend your day off doing this," Janna protested, when Michael appeared at the door of Cabin One on Saturday morning. "You and Ian could go to town or something. Have some fun."

Michael stepped into the cabin anyway, a tool belt slung low at his waist, his denim shirtsleeves rolled back. He looked so competent, so masculine, that she just wanted to stop and stare.

"We'll go to town later. I promised we'd help, and I've gotten back too late the last few nights to do anything." He smiled, but his eyes were weary, and she knew he had to be exhausted. She hadn't seen his patrol car arrive until almost nine o'clock on Thursday and Friday, and then he'd gone out into the timber on surveillance.

"Really, this could wait," she said when Ian followed him to the wobbly kitchen table with an armload of tools. "I could just start cleaning up some of the other cabins and get these repairs done later."

A sudden breeze stirred up the dust on the floor. She tried to hold back a sneeze, but failed. "Sorry— you could probably find me anywhere on the property by listening to me sneeze."

"It is handy," Michael said with a twinkle in his eye. "You should probably let us do the heavy cleaning, too."

Janna laughed. "And miss all this fun? Not on your life."

"Then at least let us tackle some repairs. The sooner this cabin is done, the sooner you'll have more paying guests." Michael looked down at the legal pad in his hand. "I've already made a list. We've got to fix this table. Replace the countertops in the kitchen and bath. Repair some of the cupboard doors…and hang a new exterior door. I figure we can get it done in a couple days, easy. Did you pick up a new door at the lumberyard?"

"I drove up to Jackson yesterday, and all of the supplies you need are in our truck." Janna surveyed the dark little cabin, envisioning how it would look with new cherry-red countertops and bright-red-and-white gingham curtains. She'd already ordered pretty patchwork quilts for the bedroom, and linens for the bath and kitchen. The image made her smile. "Just tell me what to do."

He thought for a minute. "We can handle the carpentry, if you want to do something else. Stop back now and then, though, in case we have questions."

"Good enough." She stayed to watch them, though, entranced by Michael's loving patience with his son.

After they set up some sawhorses on the porch, Michael helped Ian measure boards and cut several lengths of pine, then showed him how to brace the table high underneath, where the legs and top met.

Perspiration formed on Ian's forehead and he bit his lower lip as he awkwardly managed the screws and screwdriver. He repeatedly dropped the screws and had to search the floor for them, and as the minutes passed Janna could see the tension increasing in the stiff set of his shoulders.

When the last leg of the table was braced, Ian sat back with a gusty sigh, his face etched with relief.

"Good job, son." Michael clapped him on the back. "This sort of thing isn't easy the first time. Let's set 'er up and see how we did."

They stood and flipped the table over, and Michael grabbed the edge. "Solid as a rock. Perfect!" He ran a practiced hand over the top surface. "You know, this would be a pretty table if we stripped and sanded it. What do you think?"

Ian stared at it with something akin to horror, probably imagining endless hours of work. *"Today?"*

"For now I'd rather just go for the basics," Janna said, "so I can get this place up and running. I can do the refinishing this winter."

Ian's shoulders slumped with relief. "So, are we done yet?"

"Nope. Next, the cupboards." Michael sauntered over to test the doors, one by one, making a chalk mark on the ones needing repair. "It's a good feeling, when you can work hard and really see what you've accomplished. This should be fun."

The boy looked so restless that Janna took pity on him. "You know what? I've got a pitcher of lemonade up in the fridge at the lodge," she said. "I'll bet you and your dad would enjoy some. Could you run up and get it?"

He nodded and took off so fast that Janna laughed. "I'm not sure carpentry is his cup of tea."

"And now that he's escaped, I'm probably not going to get him back anytime soon." Michael frowned at her, though she caught a twinkle in his eye. "Sooo… want to help me get these cupboard doors off?"

"My pleasure." She picked up a screwdriver and started at one end of the row of cupboards, while he started at the other. "I enjoyed watching you work with Ian," she said after a few minutes.

Michael deftly released a warped door from its rusted hinges and set it on the floor. "I figure it might help with his dexterity and the strength in his hands. It might even be a creative outlet someday. He…lost a bright future in that accident."

"Future?" Curious, she looked down the row of cupboards at him.

He worked on another hinge, his grip on the screw-driver turning his knuckles white. "Ian was something of a prodigy. At sixteen his acrylics hung in a Chicago gallery, and two sold for five figures. Just before the accident, he was accepted into one of the most selective art schools in New York." Michael's voice roughened. "I suppose he didn't mention it, though. The whole situation is still hard on him."

"But he still has that talent. It's innate, isn't it? If he tries—"

"He can barely write. Trying anything beyond that just fills him with rage, and now he's refusing to continue therapy." Michael braced his palms on the counter and bowed his head. "It breaks my heart to see it, because there's not a thing I can do for him except pray—and so far, those prayers haven't been answered."

Ian strode back to the lodge, his hands thrust deep in his pockets, his eyes still burning from the frustration of trying to awkwardly wield that stupid screwdriver.

His fingers curled around the old knife that he still carried in his pocket every day, and he jerked it out, tempted to throw it way out into the woods where Dad would never see it. But after being a huge disappointment—a failure—in so many ways, what would one more thing matter? Ignoring Dad's orders to stay near the lodge that day was nothing compared to everything else Ian had done.

Trudging up the front steps of the lodge, he jerked

open the screen door and stalked inside after the lemonade Janna wanted. He paused, uncertain where to look. In the big kitchen meant for the restaurant area? The private quarters?

The old lady, Claire, stuck her head out of a hallway leading to the family quarters, glared at him and slammed the door shut…so that probably wasn't an option.

From over by the fireplace, Rylie looked around the edge of a big leather chair. Her face brightened. "Ian! You did come!"

Guilt slithered through his stomach at her obvious joy. He hadn't come to see her once since she'd gotten hurt…but maybe it was that same feeling of guilt that kept him away. If he hadn't selfishly hurried up the trail and left her behind, nothing bad would have happened.

It was just one more time that he'd been a total jerk and caused someone a lot of pain.

"Uh…hi." He lifted a shoulder, suddenly feeling awkward and out of place. "Your mom said I should come get some lemonade."

Rylie's face fell. "Oh." She pointed toward the double doors leading into the restaurant. "It's probably in the big kitchen. Go through there."

Feeling even worse, he tried to think of something else to say. Everyone here had to hate him, after he had so thoughtlessly left Rylie on the trail.

He made himself cross the room. "So…whatcha doing?"

"Nothin'." She gave a weary sigh and closed the oversize spiral notebook laying in her lap. "It's sorta boring, 'cause I'm not good on my crutches yet."

He took a second look at the notebook. Art paper. The cheaper stuff, to be sure, but still his heart twisted and his fingers itched to take the pencil she held—as if his hands had a mind of their own.

As if, in this lifetime, he could ever draw again.

She withdrew a little at the expression on his face, so he made himself smile and ask to see her drawings, knowing that her childish sketches would probably intensify the deep gnawing feeling in his gut.

She hesitated, then shyly opened it to the first page.

"It's my dog, Maggie," she ventured shyly. "I know it's not very good. And this is Aunt Tessa's horse…"

She flipped through several more sketches, and it wasn't until the fourth page that Ian remembered to breathe.

The drawings were just what he'd expected of someone who was nine. Nothing special. But the scent of the paper and graphite hit him like a wave of intense homesickness—powerful, overwhelming. The ache blossomed in his chest and grew until it felt as if he would explode.

"Is s-something wrong?"

He heard the tremble in her voice but couldn't form a response. He blinked. Stared. Then closed his eyes and remembered a thousand early sketches of his own. His excitement when Mom had started taking him for lessons at the Art Institute. The thrill of learning and growing, and at hearing the murmured praise of passersby when his projects were posted on the display board in the hall.

Her lower lip trembled as she closed the book. "I know," she whispered, her eyes downcast. "I'm not very good at drawing."

He shook off his memories. "Yes you are, Rylie. I was just, um, surprised. I didn't expect—"

He broke off on a sob that came out of nowhere, over all that he'd lost. The skill and talent that had made him special. That had filled him with joy.

And whenever he inadvertently allowed himself to remember what had been, the wrenching guilt and grief over his mother was soon to follow.

"I…I gotta go." He spun around and hurried for the door.

"But the lemonade—"

He didn't go back. He couldn't answer. He just ran for his cabin, ignoring the screaming tendons in his bad leg and praying Dad wasn't there, so he could be alone.

The cabin was dark. Cool. Quiet.

He rushed through the combination living and kitchen area to his bedroom. Slammed the door and flung himself onto the bed just as his hot tears started to fall. *I never cry. I never cry.*

A quiet thud came from just outside his door. Then another. With it came the eerie realization that he was not alone. His heart lodged in his throat.

"Dad?" he said softly. "Is that you?"

A floorboard squeaked. The hinges of the cabin's screen door squealed faintly, as if being slowly, slowly opened.

"Dad?" he whispered again.

But the only reply was the sound of a twig snapping, the faint rustle of leaves outside the cabin.

And the thundering of his heart.

"I don't like leaving all of you here alone," Michael said. "If it wasn't for the Monday-night city council meeting, I wouldn't go. It's one of the requirements of my job."

"I'm a big girl," Janna said firmly. "I can handle things here—and I can also call for help, if need be. We'll keep Ian up at the lodge until you get back, but I'm sure everything will be fine."

He stared over her shoulder at the lane that meandered up the hill to the cabins. "I still don't like it. If Ian was right, someone was in our cabin on Saturday in broad daylight, and I'll bet it's no coincidence that someone tampered with Claire's tires."

That was certainly true. The wrecker guys had figured it had taken about a half hour for the tires to deflate—which meant the damage had probably been done when Claire had stopped to check on her cattle. She would have been on Snow Canyon Ranch land, not far from the lodge.

Still, Janna knew she could hardly expect Michael

to babysit them all day and night. She gestured toward the door. "You're forgetting that I'm a ranch girl. I grew up shooting coyotes, and the gun rack in my mother's pickup was never empty. She probably shot more varmints than I could count over the years. We had to protect our calves."

He didn't look convinced.

"Go. You said they were discussing budget cuts on law enforcement tonight. Heaven knows what they'll decide if you aren't there to speak up."

"You'll lock the doors and windows?"

"Scout's honor."

"Keep everyone inside?"

"Of course."

"Call me every half hour?"

She shooed him down the steps of the lodge, though inwardly she was warmed by his concern. "That's going a little far. See you back here—" she glanced at her watch "—around ten?"

"Or earlier." He jogged out to his patrol car and opened the door, but turned back before climbing inside. "We're going to get to the bottom of all of this trouble before Ian and I move to town, Janna. I promise you."

She watched him drive away, his car nearly obscured by the cloud of dust it raised, and felt a small, empty place in her chest when he was out of sight.

He and Ian had dutifully worked on Cabin One all weekend, while she'd gone up to Cabin Ten to start clearing out all the rubble in that one. Once the piles of whiskey bottles and tacky magazines were hauled out, the cabin was in surprisingly good condition, so it was next on her list. And with Lauren Young starting work tomorrow she could make even faster progress.

All good—though Michael and Ian's eventual departure would definitely be a sad ending to the summer. Once the plumbing and rewiring was finished in their house on the edge of Wolf Creek, the roofers would start, and then Michael would start some of the smaller projects inside.

Even though the number of lodge guests would be growing, she knew it would seem like a very lonely place after the two of them were gone.

No longer feeling quite so upbeat, she went back into the lodge and dutifully locked all the windows and doors, pulling shades and blinds as she went.

She found Claire dozing in a recliner in her bedroom, so she quietly locked the windows, then tiptoed out. Out in the lobby of the lodge, Ian was playing a handheld video game, and Rylie bent studiously over her drawing tablet. Maggie snored softly in front of the flickering warmth of the fireplace.

Ian put his game down and leaned over to look at Rylie's picture. His brows drew together as he pointed to several places and muttered something to her. He was *coaching* her? Until now, he'd been wrapped up in himself—with good reason—but this could be a promising sign.

Delighted, Janna settled at a table in the corner and started working on her latest stack of bills, glancing at the kids now and then. Sure enough, Rylie beamed up at Ian a moment later, then went back to her drawing.

Suddenly the door to the family's wing of the lodge flew open and bounced against the wall with a resounding crack. Startled, Janna launched to her feet at the sight of Claire standing in the doorway, her robe hanging off one shoulder and her hair disheveled.

"The shotgun—where is it?" she demanded as she strode into the lobby. She rapidly scanned the room, as if expecting to find one hanging on the wall. "I need it. *Now*."

Rylie and Ian both jumped, then turned to look at Janna, their eyes wide.

"Um, Mom," Janna soothed as she hurried over to Claire. Was she delusional? "Everything's fine."

"There's a bear outside. I can *hear* it," Claire snapped. "And unless you want it ravaging your trash cans, you'd best scare it off—or I will."

"I don't think—" Janna stilled. Now she could hear some sort of ruckus outside, too—filtering down the long hallway of the north wing.

But the distant sounds were coming from the direction of the cabins, not the well-secured trash cans outside the kitchen door.

"Just leave it be, Mom. It can't do much harm."

Claire gave her a look of utter disdain. "Give me a rifle or a shotgun if you're afraid, city girl."

There were weapons in the lodge, but they were safely locked away, thank goodness. Only Janna had the key.

She lifted her cell phone from her pocket and speed-dialed Michael, spoke to him briefly, then ended the connection. "No one is going out in the dark to confront a bear, Mom. That just doesn't make sense."

"In my day I handled a lot worse than this."

Ian and Rylie were now staring at the two of them, their faces pale.

Janna forced a calm smile. "I'm sure you did, but we're still staying inside."

If it wasn't a bear, it could be something far worse. And there was no way she'd let anyone take that chance.

TEN

Janna fingered the key to the gun case—one of many keys on a ring in her pocket. The noise outside probably *was* just a bear looking for food. Maybe one of the kids had left a candy bar or half-eaten sandwich by one of the cabins, and the scent had lured a passing sow and her cubs.

Still, Janna mentally counted the strides it would take to reach that gun case, the motions required to unlock it, and load ammo into her favorite old Remington. Three minutes, tops, and she'd be armed and ready for anything that tried to break into the house.

Those steps became a constant, silent litany running through her head, because if anything tried to come through the door, it wouldn't be a bear. Only a two-footed predator would try that kind of assault.

So between planning each move she'd need to make, she lectured herself on facing off against another human being. Could she do it? Could she pull the trigger?

One glance at her frightened daughter and Ian, whose freckles now stood out in sharp relief against his pale face, and she knew she could do anything to defend these children—even if it meant facing the consequence of nightmares for the rest of her life.

"Lord, please let it be just some old, moth-eaten bear rambling around outside…and make him just wander away," she prayed quietly. "And please, Lord, protect us from all harm. In Your blessed name we pray, Amen."

"Amen," Rylie echoed.

Ian shifted uncomfortably in his chair, but didn't chime in. "I could go out and chase it away," he blurted after an awkward pause. "I'm not afraid of some stupid bear."

"You'll do no such thing." Janna smiled at him to soften her words. "Though I do appreciate your offer."

He wouldn't be that foolish, but Janna hadn't been too sure about Clair. Knowing that her unpredictable mother might just go out the private entrance un-armed and defenseless in sheer defiance, Janna had insisted she stay in the main area of the lodge with everyone else.

So now Claire sat in an easy chair by the fireplace, impatiently flipping through the stack of ranch mag-azines Janna had brought to her. Occasionally, she looked up and fixed Janna with an irritable look that spoke volumes, even though Claire had refused to say another word.

All four of them sat up and listened intently at the first, faint sound of tires crunching up the lane.

"That's Dad—I know it is," Ian announced as he rushed to a window and peered out, male bravado once again ringing in his voice.

A second later Janna's cell phone rang.

"I'm here," Michael said. "But I'm going on up to the cabins to take a look around. Just sit tight."

"A-alone? In the dark?" Janna bit her lip, imagining how many dangers could be lurking in the darkness. Unseen, until it was too late. "Wait until daylight at least."

He chuckled softly, his easy confidence reassuring her in a way no words could have. "This is my job. I don't take chances."

"But—"

"I have a spotlight on my car. I'll be back in a few minutes."

She held on to the cell phone with both hands long after he disconnected, and joined Ian at the window. The headlights of the patrol car swung wide, sweeping an arc of illumination across the lodge. Then the vehicle slowly headed up the lane, its spotlight penetrating the rows of trees surrounding the first couple of cabins.

When the taillights disappeared over the first rise, Ian looked over at her. "You look worried, but my dad knows what he's doing."

Smiling at the pride in his voice, she reached over

and gave him a one-armed hug. "I'm very glad you're both living here, honey."

At the gentle endearment, he seemed to melt against her, as if he were starving for a motherly touch, but then he stiffened and awkwardly pulled away. "It's cool here. Better than I thought, I guess."

She grinned. "I feel exactly the same way. Especially after you and your dad worked so hard on that cabin last weekend. Did your dad tell you that I want to pay you?"

"Uh…" he shifted uncomfortably. "I can't take it. It wouldn't be right."

"I think it's only fair," she countered.

"He's the one you should pay, if anyone. At least he knows what he's doing."

"He refused my money, too." She burst into laughter at Ian's smug expression, which told her that she'd just made his point for him—just as he'd planned. "Stinker."

He sauntered back to his chair and video game, but the air in the room had changed, and her heart warmed as she watched him settle sideways in the chair, his gangly legs draped over the armrest.

A connection at last. They'd finally communicated without all of the walls that Ian had built around himself. He'd let it happen, she realized, because he'd seen how worried she was and had wanted to help.

The perceptive, thoughtful side of him touched her heart.

She glanced at the clock on the mantel. "Time for bed, Rylie, but I'm going to get your pajamas and keep you down here for a while longer. You can brush your teeth down here, too."

By the time she'd finished Rylie's bedtime routines and settled her on a sofa with some blankets, Michael was walking up the front steps of the lodge.

Relieved at his safe return, she met him on the porch and closed the front door behind her for more privacy. "Did you see anything?"

In the shadows, his face appeared weary and drawn. "Nothing moving out there now. But you definitely had a guest. Several, I'd guess."

Janna's blood chilled. "What did they do?"

"You were working on the farthest cabin over the weekend, right?"

"I cleaned out the trash and started emptying out the cupboards." She shuddered, remembering the thick layer of mouse droppings on the shelves. Even the floors were thick with them, and her first assault with pine disinfectant hadn't begun to obliterate the smell of decay and mustiness. For that job, she'd worn a face mask as much for the dust as for the risk of hanta virus exposure from the droppings.

"You locked it up afterward? Didn't go back for a wild party with your friends?"

"As if." She managed a nervous laugh. "Of course I locked it."

She could sense that he didn't want to scare her.

That he was searching for the right words, but his hesitation made her tension escalate all the more.

"Cabin Ten was unlocked. The doors and windows were wide-open. Looks like someone had a major pizza party, because three or four greasy takeout boxes were thrown inside, and I found more along the trail."

"A *party?*" Stunned, she thought back to the noises she'd heard earlier tonight. There'd been no music. No sounds of voices and laughter. And who on earth would hike this far from the main highway for something like that? A sudden thought hit her. "You said pizza boxes. No beverages containers?"

He canted his head. "Exactly. No beer cans or empty liquor bottles. No pop cans. No paper cups."

"But then why—" she took a deep breath. "It was bait."

"And it worked. There are bears all over these mountains, and they've got an amazing sense of smell. They love to congregate at landfills.

"At least one must've followed the scent of that pizza and wasn't afraid to walk right in the open door of an empty, isolated cabin. Someone probably tossed leftover pieces of pizza all over, because the furniture is torn up, and some cupboard doors are hanging loose. The window screens are torn…even the refrigerator is tipped over. I'd say its door is twisted beyond repair."

She sank into the porch swing and took a shaky breath. "This is just *crazy.*"

He pulled up a chair and sat in front of her, his eyes dark and somber as he took her hand between both of his. "There was something else, too, Janna, and I'd say it's a clear warning. Someone shot a coyote and dragged it inside. There's blood all over the floor. I'll bring the other officers out here at daylight, and we'll comb the area for clues."

Her stomach tightened into a painful knot. "But why would anyone go to all this trouble, when he could've—" she swallowed hard "—just broken into the lodge and come after us?"

"Think about it. Someone has been out here searching for something. Probably the killer, afraid he left evidence behind. Afraid it'll be found, now that the lodge is reopening and more people will be here."

"Those new holes being dug out in the woods. The guy lurking around your cabin. But my mother's tires—"

"Logically, not a coincidence. He's escalating. First the tires and now this—he probably hopes to scare you away. If you give up on opening the lodge, he doesn't have to worry."

"'Escalating' suddenly sounds like a very bad word." She tried to calm her erratic heartbeat. "Maybe you should take Ian and move into that house of yours in town. Even if it isn't ready, it's still safer than here."

"But without plumbing or electricity," Michael said with a wry smile. "I do want Ian to be with you at the lodge when I'm not here, though—until we figure out who's doing this."

"There's the guy I glimpsed in the woods."

"A strong possibility."

"The man in town who threatened me, a few weeks ago."

"True."

"Or…it could just be a bunch of teenagers, on a lark—getting their jollies from trying to scare someone."

Michael hesitated on that one. "I doubt it, but I've already got my deputies asking questions around town, and I'll be following up on that, as well."

A chill of fear made her shiver. She turned sharply and discovered Claire standing in the shadows just beyond the porch steps. Watching them.

"Mom," she said faintly. "I didn't hear you come out."

"I went for a walk," Claire snapped. "Went out the other door, not that it's a concern of yours."

"Oh, Mom—this isn't a good time for you to be wandering in the dark. Please, go inside."

Claire snorted. "You're the one who's worried, not me. No one messes with the McAllisters around here."

Michael's eyes were deep with understanding when Janna looked up and caught his gaze. They both knew there would be no way to convince Claire of anything else, and trying would just start another argument.

"By the way," Claire added. "I want to know what fool threatened you."

Janna hesitated, but Michael nodded in encouragement. "A middle-aged guy. Tall and lean, dressed like a ranch hand. Had a low, mean tone in his voice."

Claire didn't miss a beat. "Square jaw. Crooked nose."

Janna nodded.

"And dumb as an ox." Claire made a sound of disgust as she came up the porch steps. "Lowell Haskins. Hired him on as a foreman—fired him six months later and warned him to never set foot on this place again."

"Wh-what did he do?"

"I told you before, I never put up with boozers or brawlers, and he was both. He fought with some cowboy at a street dance and sent the guy to the hospital. Over some floozy, I heard."

"Did he serve time?"

"The guy wouldn't press charges, and the fool sheriff let him go." Claire's voice conveyed satisfaction. "But I made sure Lowell paid his dues. There wasn't anyone in the county who'd hire him after that."

Janna waited until Claire went back inside, then shook her head. "That's certainly good news. My mother made a lifelong enemy of a man known for drinking and violence."

"Though in her world, she did what she thought was right to protect her fellow ranchers. That took courage."

"I…suppose that's true."

Michael smiled, his teeth flashing white in the darkness. "And now we have the name of a potential suspect. Tomorrow, I can start checking on where Lowell was this evening. I'll also check the alibis of any teens who've been troublemakers in the past, too—just to make sure tonight's incident wasn't just some teenage prank. Who knows? Maybe your problems are nearly over."

"Oh, Mrs. McAllister," Lauren breathed, surveying the damage in Cabin Ten. Stepping farther inside, she scooped back her long, straight black hair and stared at the torn mattresses and ripped screens. "This is awful!" Her eyes dropped to the dark, still-damp areas on the floor and one wall. "And what is *that?*"

It was only fair to tell her. As a new employee, she needed to know exactly what risks she might face. Her eyes widened when Janna told her about all that had been happening at the lodge.

"I took care of the coyote blood yesterday," Janna said quietly. "With gloves, detergent and a strong bleach solution."

Lauren shivered. "Wow."

"I haven't had a chance to get back in here until today, but this is my next project." Janna watched her expression closely. "If you have any hesitation about working here, there'll be no hard feelings whatsoever. I'll pay you for a full day's work today, even if you leave right now."

She needn't have worried. The girl was seventeen, still filled with youthful energy and a certain amount of naiveté.

"I think it sounds *exciting*," Lauren exclaimed. "And anyway, the cops will catch the bad guys before long."

Janna smothered a smile. "I can't guarantee it—but you'll be here during the day, at any rate, and broad daylight ought to be pretty quiet."

"So I'll be mostly helping you clean up the place, then?"

"Just for now. I've got to get all of the cabins open and ready for guests. After that, I'll need you as a cabin maid, and for watching over the place if I have to run errands. My mother—" Janna hesitated "—is older, so I hate to leave her alone. I've also got a nine-year-old daughter. With you here, I can start riding again. I love the solitude, but haven't dared leave without someone else here."

"Cool. So where do I start?" Before Janna could even answer, Lauren strode into the first bedroom and eyed the stained, ripped mattress. "Eeeeuw! Right here, I think. Can you help me lug this thing out?"

Janna caught up with her and gingerly took the other end. "There might be mice," she warned.

"Raised 'em for my snakes when I was in high school. Not a problem." Their eyes met, and Lauren broke into laughter. "Um, that usually isn't a big sell-ing point on a date."

The past two weeks had been harder than Janna had even realized, but now she felt some of that weight lift from her shoulders. "You are definitely the right girl for this job, Lauren. Welcome to Snow Canyon!"

ELEVEN

His law enforcement duties drew him to all locations of the county, but Michael's heart was back at Wolf Creek—where someone still threatened the safety of Janna and her family.

The fact that he hadn't been able to make much progress on the case burned like fire in his gut and kept him awake at night.

Since the vandalism at the cabin on Monday, he'd spent every spare moment questioning people about Lowell Haskins, and asking about any local high school guys who might belong to the most-likely-to-offend crowd. He stayed out late at night, watching for the elusive stranger Janna had seen out in the woods.

So far he'd hit nothing but dead ends.

He'd found no more evidence of digging out in the woods, and had seen no one lurking out there. By Wednesday he'd been able to talk to four hulking Wolf Creek area high school seniors who'd all been in minor trouble over the years, but every one of them had been over in Salt Grass for the stock car races on Sunday night, in school on Monday, and had family or job alibis on Monday evening.

Fifteen minutes ago he'd received a call from one of his deputies, who'd seen Lowell Haskins walking into a tavern outside of town. Michael had turned it into a hot call—lights and sirens until just a mile away—to make sure he got there in time.

He didn't have to worry.

The place was dark. Smoky. Lit mostly by the faint, fluorescent glow of the beer signs hanging over the bar. Even at three in the afternoon it smelled of stale beer, sweat and desperation.

A couple of scrawny, unshaven guys sat alone, their forearms resting on the tables in front of them, nursing bottles of cheap whiskey.

Two others sat at the bar. Neither of them turned around at the harsh flood of sunlight that poured in when Michael opened the door. The bartender did a double take at his uniform and took a half step back, his hands raised in the universal gesture for I-don't-want-any-trouble.

Michael zeroed in on the guy at the left with thinning salt-and-pepper hair and wrinkled, sun-cured skin at the back of his neck. "Lowell?"

The bartender nodded and moved to the far end of the bar.

Lowell met Michael's eyes in the mirror behind a row of liquor bottles and beer taps on the back wall.

He sat rock still for a few moments. Then he took a long draw on his cigarette and flicked the ashes into an overflowing ashtray in front of him.

He turned slowly. "I done nothing wrong."

"Didn't say you did. I just have a few questions."

Lowell studied him, his eyes narrowed. "You're the cop who's in with the McAllisters."

"Excuse me?"

"Gotta be interesting living out at ol' lady McAllister's place." His mouth twisted. "Those daughters of hers are lookers, but she's a piece of work."

"I understand you were a foreman out there."

Lowell turned back to the glass in front of him and downed it in one long swallow. "Yeah. Big mistake."

"Good job?"

"Like I said, big mistake."

Michael hooked a boot on the foot rail and rested an elbow on the bar. Bared his teeth in a smile. "Work around here?"

Only a single twitch of the man's eyelid hinted at his sudden tension. "You probably know the answer to that already, *deppity*."

"Maybe I don't believe everything I hear."

Lowell's gaze slid away. "I do odd jobs—when I can get 'em."

"Were you in this county during the last few weeks?"

"Now and then."

Michael's interest ratcheted up another notch. "Here—as in Wolf Creek?"

A brief tip of the head. "Carson Ranch, a few days working calves. Before that, over in Harris County."

"What about Sunday and Monday?"

Lowell's hand tightened around his glass. "Why?"

"Curious."

Lowell swung around on his bar stool and cursed. "I cain't see you coming all the way out here to ask if I was havin' a nice time. Is this where I oughta ask for a lawyer?"

Michael shrugged affably. "Seemed like a pretty easy question, unless you were someplace you shouldn't have been."

The following silence was laden with resentment and simmering anger.

"My dad's place," Lowell finally bit out. "I was there, okay?"

"Both nights?"

"Ask him. Harvey Haskins—owns the trailer court south of town two miles. Lives in the blue-and-white, back row."

"Thanks. I just might." Michael nodded to the bartender lingering at the far end of the bar and turned to leave, but stopped and looked over his shoulder at Lowell. "When was the last time you were on McAllister land?"

Lowell stiffened. "Four, five years…unless I maybe wandered over the line while hunting."

"Thanks." Michael strode out into the sunshine, welcoming the fresh, clean air.

It wouldn't take Lowell a minute to call his father and warn him about what to say, but the trip wouldn't be a waste of time. What a guy tried to hide was often there in the uneasy flicker of his gaze. The subtle tension. Nuances in his voice and a hesitation in his answers.

And Lowell had certainly telegraphed fear from the moment he saw a uniform come into the bar.

Michael had driven by the trailer park many times. He'd figured that sooner or later his job would bring him to this place in the dark of night on a domestic-abuse call. A shooting. Drugs.

There was a pretty trailer park tucked into the pines on the other side of town, where the residents had planted flowers, put up little white fences around their plots and all but waxed and polished the lane meandering through the property.

This park, on the other hand, was the kind of place where trailers came to die. A boneyard of rusted, crumbling 1960s models, where trash accumulated everywhere but in the Dumpsters, and old men in dirty undershirts sat on their stoops sucking on cigarette stubs.

But no one sat on the steps of the blue-and-white in the back row.

Michael stood to one side and rapped on the door. Waited a minute, then rapped again. "Anyone home?"

A long silence, then a harsh, wheezy cough.

He unsnapped the safety strap over the butt of his gun.

"Sir, are you okay? Can I come in?"

At a mumbled reply, he eased the door open with caution born of far too many years in homicide. The horizontal blinds were all drawn, leaving just razor-thin blades of sunlight to cut through the haze of cigarette smoke.

It took a second for Michael's eyes to adjust. Longer to force himself to step inside and breathe the stale air.

Unshaven male. Easily one-ninety to two hundred pounds. Late seventies. Balding. A stained T-shirt stretched across his massive, protruding stomach. Oxygen tubing dangled from the prongs in his nose.

"Maybe not a good idea to be smoking with that oxygen," Michael said mildly.

The man uttered a single curse. "Look around and tell me why I should care." His voice was breathy, and the effort sent him into a round of heavy coughing.

Emphysema, Michael guessed. A healthy lifestyle apparently wasn't a priority in the Haskins clan. "Do you have anyone from the county doing home visits here?"

"Got no need. Don't want nobody comin' in here." Harvey's gaze sharpened, though he had to draw in a couple of deeper breaths before trying to speak again. "What do you want?"

"I just wondered when you last saw your son, Lowell."

Harvey leaned forward in his recliner, his eyes widening in alarm. "Is he all right?"

"Downing whiskey at a tavern an hour ago. I'm not sure if you'd consider that 'all right,' since it was before noon." Michael glanced at the dirty dishes piled in the sink. Beer cans overflowing a trash can. No land or cell phone in sight. "I just need to know when he was here last, and for how long."

Harvey sank back into his chair, his breathing labored. "Dunno. All weekend, I guess. He comes and goes."

"He's out at night?"

"Stays in, when he's here." A dull flush crept up the man's wattled neck. "Helps me…if I have to get to the can."

"Can you phone him whenever you need him to stay with you?"

Harvey snorted. "Could if I had a phone."

"Just one last thing. What do you know about the McAllisters?"

Anger flashed in the old man's eyes. "Liars, every one of 'em." He raised his hand and made a sweeping gesture around his cramped trailer. "Weren't for them, Lowell woulda had a good job all these years. He'd own a decent place and I'd be with him, not in this sewer."

"What happened?"

"Claire McAllister." He spat out the name as if it tasted vile. "Get on the wrong side of her, and you can kiss your life goodbye. No one in the county would hire Lowell permanent, after what she said about him."

Exactly what she'd admitted doing. "So why didn't he move on?"

"I can't sell the trailer—couldn't ever git it up to code." Harvey's eyes glistened. "He stayed around to help me, I guess. But that just means we'll both die poor."

Michael had wanted to bring Janna good news. Frustrated, he pulled to a stop by his cabin but stayed in the car, the door open and one wrist draped over the wheel.

He'd seen nothing but honest anger and bitterness in Harvey's eyes. Today's investigation didn't eliminate Lowell as a suspect, but it did put him lower on the list.

A phone call to the county health department put Harvey on a list as well.

His living conditions were deplorable, his health precarious. The county's visiting nurses would be paying him a visit in a few days to assess him as an older adult in need of assistance, so he could get the help he needed.

Michael sighed as he stepped out of the car. There was something missing—some piece to this puzzle that was still eluding him.

Janna called his name, and he turned to find her coming up the lane with an armload of linens.

She wore no makeup, but with her sunglasses perched on her head and her hair drawn back in a silky ponytail that swung with every step, she looked so fresh and pretty that he once again felt that familiar warmth build in his heart.

"These are for you," she said. "I can set them inside."

He reached for her burden instead. "I'll take them. How's everything?"

"Good news and bad. It's starting to be the story of my life."

But she grinned, and he couldn't help but smile right back. At the end of every day, during the long drive back to Snow Canyon, he found himself looking forward to seeing her, and when he did, his day felt complete.

He shifted the weight of the linens in his arms. "What happened?"

"Lauren is wonderful. She's a hard worker and really sweet to Rylie and Claire."

"Claire?" he tried to picture Claire accepting anyone being "sweet" toward her and failed.

Janna laughed. "Not baby-talk sweet. She jokes with her, and doesn't take any guff. I think my mom admires her already, and having Lauren here meant that I actually got to go riding this morning, *alone*. The beauty and solitude of these mountains is beyond description. I'm going every morning, from now on."

"I thought you were going to stay close to the lodge."

"I've been riding this land all my life." She waved off his concern. "There's a rifle scabbard on my saddle, and I can handle myself. Anyway, early morning has to be pretty safe, don't you think?"

"I wouldn't count on it," he warned. "Promise you'll be careful."

"I won't do anything foolish, believe me. Just some nice rides on my old stomping grounds, that's all."

"You mentioned some bad news?"

She made a face. "The entire septic system for cabins Seven through Ten. With the rugged terrain here, they share a separate system, and it isn't adequate per the current environmental codes. Not exactly where I wanted to sink a few thousand dollars, believe me."

"The county was out here to check?"

"I contacted them last week. They went over their old records, then sent a guy out this morning to take a look. Those cabins can't be used until the system is replaced. I even talked to Wade Hollister to see if there was anything we could do legally to open them on an interim basis. He said no."

Michael whistled. "How long will that take?"

"I've been calling," she said glumly. "So far no dice until the end of July. Worse, Wade says it's hard to pass those inspections. The county guys come out at every stage and have to sign off on them. What they don't like has to be done over. Wade said that if it proves impossibly expensive, he'll offer me a secretarial job." She rolled her eyes. "So, tell me about *your* day."

"A couple of minor accidents. Domestic dispute. Sheriff Brownley called, wondering how things were going."

"Anything on our troubles up here?"

"Just a minute." He took the linens into the cabin, where Ian was immersed in a book and came right back out. "Let's walk up the hill…might be a little more private."

They strolled up the lane, and when she slipped her arm through his, it seemed as natural and right as the warmth of the sun overhead and the crisp scent of pine.

"I found Lowell Haskins, and I also talked to his father. They both hold a grudge against your mother, but it sounds like Lowell has an alibi during this last incident."

"I was afraid of that. It would have been just too easy."

"So I've been trying to think through the possibilities. Who else would've been in the area back then—and is still around, frightened by the possibility of discovery? A professional hit would have been neat. Perfectly handled, with no evidence carelessly left behind. The shooter would have been brought in from some urban area—where he'd have more business—and would have disappeared immediately afterward."

He felt her shudder against his arm. "Go on."

"This case bears the marks of an amateur. Someone who panicked, maybe. Who neither planned the kill nor thought ahead about the disposal of the remains. With the vast Rockies all around, luring the intended victim to a far more remote area for instant burial would have been the logical choice—and a lot easier, if the killer had stopped to think."

"So it was probably a crime of passion. A moment of rage."

"Exactly. The killer and victim were probably in the vicinity for other reasons. Hikers, maybe. A couple who'd come out to these abandoned buildings for a liaison, or a party that got out of hand. Could have been campers vacationing here or locals…but my money is still on the latter. Because someone around here is afraid and really doesn't want you to turn up more evidence."

TWELVE

Ian sat in the shadowed corner of the cabin's porch, his feet propped on the porch railing and his chair tipped back.

At this altitude, the crisp early-morning air warmed rapidly beneath the fierce mid-June sun, and he'd already shucked his fleece pullover and jeans in favor of shorts and a ratty, cropped-off T-shirt. They were clothes he would never have worn at home, where someone might have seen his scars. But now Dad was at work, Janna would be off working in a cabin somewhere, and Rylie was mostly housebound with her broken ankle.

He idly probed at the gnarled scarring that twisted from just below his knee, up his thigh, then disappeared under the side hem of his shorts to end over his hip. Still an ugly dark pink, it contrasted sharply against his winter-pale skin.

He looked like Frankenstein, pieced together with puckers and ridges that were supposed to fade in time. It sure didn't look possible. And he couldn't even try to get a tan to help hide them, because the doctors had said his scars would look *worse*.

Scowling, he grabbed the paper bag at the side of his chair and held it in his lap, crumpling the stiff paper at the top. Rebellion and anger and fear warred inside him. *It hurt so much…so much…*

But no one was here. No one could see him fail and offer all of those stupid clichés about other things he could do instead. Or about how he'd surely get better in time.

Reaching inside, he pulled out the leather-bound sketchbook and set of Sakura pens Dad had given him a few weeks ago. He closed his eyes at the feel of the smooth paper beneath his fingertips and the scent of fine Italian leather.

These were art supplies he'd never been able to afford with his part-time job after school, supplies that silently spoke to just how much Dad hoped he'd make an effort at something he could no longer do. The oppressive weight of failure and loss settled over him like a lead blanket.

After a moment he glanced around at the empty landscape, then tore open the package of pens with his teeth and curled his stiff fingers around the barrel of one of them. The pen wobbled in his grasp. Biting his lip, he glared at his hand, channeling his frustration into forcing those muscles to tighten.

Even though he almost never prayed anymore, he

started praying now—an awkward, silent prayer. God probably wouldn't bother to listen to someone who'd ignored Him for so long, but he was asking anyway.

Ian's first try for a straight line on the paper skated off into the margin of the notebook. The second veered weakly off at an angle. Sweat trickled down his back as he forced himself to try again and again, his surgeon's words marching through his thoughts.

Loss of fine-motor control...

Hard to say at this point if it will ever fully return.

I'm sorry...sorry...sorry...

Closing his eyes, Ian leaned his head against the back of his chair with a cry of frustration.

Seeing Rylie's drawings had felt like a knife wound to his heart; they were a devastating reminder of all he'd lost. Mom had been so sure he'd end up the next Andrew Wyeth—the only artist she could remember by name.

Until now he'd let his grief and frustration build a stone wall that kept him from trying. Rylie's drawings were childish, but with coaching she could get better. What if he worked at it? Tried every single day and just didn't say anything? Could he bring back the ability he'd once had?

If he still failed, he'd be the only one who knew.

"Hey, what's up?" a cheerful voice called out.

Startled, he rocked forward in his chair, the notebook and pens scattering on the floor.

The most awesomely beautiful girl he'd ever seen in his life stood just a few feet from the porch with a bucket of cleaning supplies in her hand. *Smiling* at him.

Horror shot through him at her friendly expression, alive with curiosity. She had to have seen his bare arms and legs, and the totally gross scars that even he could barely stand to look at.

Her smile faltered. "Uh, sorry if I interrupted you."

He stared speechlessly at her, his mind completely blank.

"I'm Lauren," she added. "New employee. I was just, um, on my way to help Janna with a cabin. Guess I'll see you around." She raised a hand in a casual farewell, then turned and started up the hill.

She looked like the kind of girl who ran with the most popular kids. Ended up homecoming queen. Class president. Dated the coolest guy in school.

Even at his best, those girls never gave him a second look. Now this one had seen him at his worst—a scarred, misshapen ogre who couldn't even manage to say hello. No surprise—she certainly hadn't lingered very long, and had there been a hint of distaste in her eyes when she'd turned away. He was sure there was.

With that, he saw a glimpse of his future. Who would ever want him? He'd never be handsome. Never be the kind of guy who pretty girls would date. He'd be a curiosity and nothing more.

His humiliation was complete.

* * *

Janna rechecked Frosty's girth, then flipped the stirrup down and stepped up into the saddle. A feeling of exhilaration swept through her as she neck reined the old mare toward the network of trails to the north.

Despite Michael's warnings about going out alone, this was one thing she simply could not give up.

She'd found her old saddle in the tack room at the home place—a custom-made Balanced Ride given to her by Uncle Gray when she turned sixteen. Even after all these years, it was a perfect fit for her, and riding it brought back a flood of memories every time she started up the trail.

The old days, spent with her sisters moving cattle up to summer range. Doctoring calves. The long rides alone into the mountains, where the magnificent scenery and solitude provided balm for her soul after yet another difficult encounter with her mother.

The occasional summer horse shows, when she and Tessa had entered team pennings and had somehow managed to work so well together.

Those days were long past. Even maturity, the passage of years and all of the conference calls spent discussing Claire's situation hadn't brought back any of the camaraderie the sisters had once shared.

Tessa was in the high country on one trip after another these days. When she did stop by it was mostly to see Claire, and her visits were chilly at best. Leigh was swamped with the demands of veterinary school.

She didn't call anyone very often, and always seemed coolly indifferent. Would it ever be possible to regain what they had all lost?

Janna skirted the playground by the lodge and waved to Rylie, who stood forlornly by an open window. "You can ride when I get back," Janna called out. "I'll be back in an hour or two."

Rylie nodded somberly, then Lauren appeared at her shoulder and they both waved before turning away.

Thanks to Lauren, Janna had been able to ride for the past four mornings, and the solitude had been sheer bliss. After each ride Janna lifted Rylie into the saddle and led the old mare and child around the resort grounds.

It helped Rylie get out of the house to enjoy the sunshine, though she longed for the chance to ride on her own. Yesterday, the doctor at the hospital up in Jackson had said it would be another four or five weeks before her cast could come off.

Janna eased Frosty in a slow, rocking lope across the grassy area by the lodge and up the mouth of the trail. Chipmunks scampered across the path, and irritable squirrels scolded from the branches high overhead as she passed.

She dropped the mare into a honey-smooth jog when the trail began winding through rocky outcroppings and dark, cool stands of pines. It grew steeper, littered with rocks and slippery pebbles, and now the mare automatically slowed to a walk and picked her way carefully along what had narrowed to little more than a deer trail.

At the top of the first rise the trail opened up into a small meadow bisected by an icy mountain stream. Janna had been coming up here every day, and each time she felt her heart fill with a sense of peace and wonder at God's delicate and perfect design.

The meadow was just as it had been when she a girl. Pristine, with lush grass and a riot of early-summer wildflowers. Sunny glacier lilies. Flaming Indian paintbrush and cream colored globeflowers. Near the stream, where the earth was always damp in the spring, wild iris nodded gently in the breeze.

Frosty balked, then grudgingly waded into the knee-high stream, where Janna let her have a quick drink and watched silvery cutthroat trout dart through the water.

Rich vacationers populated the Hoback and Snake rivers using five-hundred-dollar reels and wearing fly fishing gear worth thousands of dollars, but as kids, she and her sisters had come to this secret place to fly fish in ragged shorts and sandals, using ancient equipment.

They'd prepared their catch over a fire, and nothing—not even in the finest restaurants—had ever tasted so incredibly good.

Smiling at the memory, Janna nudged Frosty with her calf and the mare splashed her way out of the stream and lunged up the opposite, rocky bank. "One more stop, old girl," she murmured, reaching down to give her a pat on the neck.

The trail rose sharply now, winding through massive boulders and clouds of snow still hiding in the shady places, then narrowed to just a few feet wide as it crossed the face of a cliff. Pebbles bounced crazily down the sheer drop-off below as Frosty passed, while above, Janna could see nothing but rough gray granite.

It was not a spot for the faint of heart or a flatlands horse.

At the top, she felt a thrill of excitement rush through her even before traversing the last quarter mile through a thick stand of sub alpine fir and Engelmann spruce.

They made the final turn—and there it was.

A sweeping, breathtaking view of the Rockies filled the horizon. Massive gray bare granite, jagged snowy peaks rising defiantly against the sky like some prehistoric monster's teeth.

Janna shook some slack in the reins and let Frosty graze on the sparse, wiry grass, then leaned back to prop a hand against the mare's broad rump, her heart humbled and filled with wonder at the magnificence of God's glory.

But now a dark, forbidding bank of clouds was edging over the peaks, bringing with it the threat of the swift, lightning-filled thunderstorms that frequented these upper ranges.

"Definitely time to head back, old girl," she said, reining Frosty back down the trail.

The mare pivoted and picked up a faster pace, clearly eager for home and knowing exactly where to go. Chuckling, Janna gave her her head until they reached the cliff, where she dropped the mare into a slow walk.

"Easy, babe," Janna murmured when they reached the most narrow stretch.

Frosty's ears suddenly flicked back and forth. She moved into a nervous little jig for a few yards, her tail lashing.

Bear? Wolves? Janna craned her neck but could see nothing behind them, nothing above.

There was no room to turn around. Reverse gear wasn't an option—the mare would likely back off the trail into the abyss below. Plus, it was far too narrow to dismount.

A silent prayer on her lips, Janna urged the mare forward one cautious step at a time, trying to avoid telegraphing her own fear to the jittery horse.

Fifty yards.

Forty.

Pebbles pinged down the wall of rock from above, bouncing crazily against the rough surface. Startled, Frosty broke into that nervous jig again. If she'd been on the flat, she'd be sidestepping, though at least she had the sense not to forget where she was.

The hair on Janna's arms stood up.

Something rumbled, cracked, and a basketball-size rock flew past Frosty's nose. The mare tried to scramble backward then more rocks fell, grazed the back of Janna's shirt and hit the mare's rump. Frosty humped her back and snorted, her feet splayed, then she lurched forward, no longer picking her careful way along the treacherous path.

The rocks kept coming—bigger and bigger, careening down the cliff with an ominous rumble, each with the velocity and mass for lethal force. Janna gripped the reins tighter, trying to hold the panicking mare back from headlong flight.

Then she looked up.

She could make out the top edge of the cliff face. A massive boulder hung over the lip. Then slowly, slowly it rotated forward, the earth giving way under its weight. A shower of pebbles and sand stung Janna's face and arms, blinding her for a split second.

An avalanche roared down from above.

Lord, please help us, she whispered frantically.

Her heart thundering in her ears, she gave Frosty her head and let the mare surge ahead, praying that the sure-footed old horse wouldn't stumble. Praying they could reach the safety of the trees ahead.

The mare made a low, guttural sound of terror and bolted, her feet slipping and sliding on the narrow ledge. Then she leaped—an ungainly, desperate jump—over a cascade of rocks sliding over the trail.

Twenty yards.

Ten.

Then they were safe in the blessed, deep shadows of the trees.

But the roar of the avalanche behind them told her just how close death had been.

Though Janna had thanked Michael profusely for helping with Cabin One and had told him he'd done more than enough, she found that he'd moved on to Cabin Two after she put Frosty back in the corral.

Tall, dark and pensive, Ian stood next to him, a mirror image of his father as Michael surveyed the exterior of the cabin, looked down at a clipboard, then peered back at the eaves and frowned. They turned as one when she approached on foot.

"Good ride?" Michael asked.

"It was—interesting."

His intent gaze scanned her from head to foot, then zeroed in on her right shoulder, where her T-shirt had ripped and a falling rock had scraped her skin. It had bled a little, welding her shirt to the wound.

"What on earth happened?"

"A little rock slide up the mountain. Caught me unaware." She smiled ruefully. "Next time I'd better pay closer attention."

"Just out of the blue."

She nodded. His voice held worlds of doubt and echoed what she'd been thinking all the way home. Coincidences happened in movies and storybooks, not in real life.

"May I?" he inclined his head toward her shoulder, then stepped closer and gently pulled the loose neckline of the T-shirt a few inches away, taking care not to disturb the wound.

His touch sent a shiver through her that had nothing at all to do with her injury, and everything to do with the subtle, growing attachment she felt for him.

He drew in a sharp breath. "You got yourself quite a scrape there—all across your shoulder blade. By tomorrow there'll be a whale of a bruise, too. Can Lauren or your mom help you with this?"

"I can get it."

He glanced over at Ian. "I think I'll have to look at this cabin later. Okay with you?"

Ian looked between them, his eyes alight with curiosity, but he just nodded and headed back to their cabin.

Michael waited until he was beyond hearing distance. "I need to see where this rock slide happened."

There was deep concern in his eyes and something else—a level of caring and connection that went beyond simple friendship. *So he feels it, too*, she thought.

"I can take you up there, if you'd like."

He shook his head in a decisive no. "Tell me where it was. I want you to stay right here."

"But—"

"Please." His voice softened. "You need to get that wound cleaned up. I promise you, your shoulder is going to be aching by tonight." A corner of his mouth tipped up. "Give me good directions, and I'm sure I can find the way."

"But you don't know the mountains like I do," she countered. "If our friend *is* up there, you'll be at a disadvantage."

His eyes twinkled. "Ah, but this sort of thing is my job. I'll bring my two-way radio and cell, though. The question is—do you have a horse I can use?"

"Frosty is tuckered out. But if you want, you can take Mopsy." The gelding, named by a ranch hand's little girl, was another old-timer from the home place. Tessa had trailered him over a few days ago so Ian and Rylie could ride once her cast was off.

"You don't have, say, a Lightning or Tornado?"

She knew he was trying to distract her with humor, and she couldn't help but smile. "Mopsy. He's a good, dependable kids' horse now, but he spent his career as a trail horse in the mountains. He'll get the job done."

"Mopsy." He gave her a pained look. "If this is a pony, I'd rather walk."

"Ohh, I think he'll suit you just fine—if you can get on him."

Michael left the barn on Mopsy—all seventeen hands of him—right after lunch. The lumbering giant of a horse was supremely dependable, and Janna had figured the two of them should be back by four at the latest.

Four o'clock passed.

Five.

At five-thirty, she started calling Michael's cell

phone, knowing that reception was unpredictable up on the mountain, but hoping that he'd at least see Missed Call on his screen.

At six, her anxiety grew and her patience dwindled. Where could he be? Anyone new to the area could get lost, but the alternatives were even worse. He'd been suspicious about the rock slide—what if he'd been caught off guard by someone up the trail?

She jogged out to the stable and cross-tied Frosty in the aisle, then dragged her saddle out of the tackroom. Michael was right—her shoulder ached, and the deep scrapes in her flesh burned beneath the thick coat of antibiotic cream and gauze bandaging.

Her muscles screamed in protest when she hoisted the saddle onto the horse's back, but in minutes she'd slung her rifle scabbard on the saddle, along with saddle bags filled with supplies, and was headed up-country at a fast jog.

At every bend in the trail she prayed that she'd find Michael on his way home, safe and sound. But there was no sign of him—not on the trail, not at her favorite meadow or beyond.

Surely she'd encounter Mopsy heading for home solo if Michael had taken a fall, but there was no sign of horse or rider…until Frosty's head jerked up, ears pricked, and she whinnied.

Janna reined the mare well off the trail and behind a thick copse of serviceberry. She eased her rifle out of the scabbard and held it across her lap—just in case.

The mare bobbed her head and snorted, dancing in place.

"Easy, babe." Crooning softly, Janna placed a hand on Frosty's neck to settle her. "Easy now. I sure hope that's your friend up the trail and not someone else."

Frosty jigged sideways, then froze with her head raised high. Now Janna could hear the clopping sound of unshod hooves, too.

A moment later Mopsy appeared.

Alone.

THIRTEEN

The forbidding bank of clouds she'd seen earlier had stalled over the peaks of the mountains for a few hours, but now they loomed overhead, and fat drops of rain started to fall.

Blinking against the rain hitting her lashes, Janna slid her rifle back in its scabbard and urged Frosty forward to snag Mopsy's reins. She looped them around her saddle horn, then rummaged in her saddlebags for a wallet-size package containing a plastic rain poncho and quickly pulled it over her head.

"Whoa—that looks really inviting! Got another one?"

Utter relief rushed through her at the sound of Michael's voice. "You bet."

He must have come through a heavier squall of rain at the higher elevation, because his shirt was soaked and plastered to his chest, and his hair was dripping water down his face. But—praise the Lord—he was walking at a good clip and appeared to be unharmed.

She gestured to a rocky overhang midway between them. "I have an extra sweatshirt, too."

Dismounting, she tied the horses to a couple of birch trees and released the saddlebags, then dashed under the ledge. "What on earth happened?"

"John Wayne's horse always stayed where he left it," Michael said with a rueful grin. "Apparently, Mopsy hasn't seen many movies. Unless they were about Houdini, because I did have him tied to a tree."

He shivered, his teeth chattering. "Take your shirt off," Janna ordered. She bent over the saddlebags and pulled out the sweatshirt, then found another poncho. "The sweatshirt's just a medium, but at least it's dry."

He peeled off his shirt and tossed it on a nearby sagebrush. The smooth, hard muscles of his chest flexed and glistened as he struggled to pull the snug sweatshirt over his wet skin. It barely brushed the belt loops of his jeans, but a moment later he'd donned the poncho.

He was still shaking, his face pale, but he smiled in gratitude. "I can't tell you how glad I am to see you," he said fervently, looking out at the pouring rain. "It would have been a long, wet walk home."

"Can't have you catching pneumonia." She peered up at the sky. "These storms are usually short, though. In an hour, the ground will be all but dry."

A bolt of lightning sizzled through the air in a blast of brilliant light, followed a split second later by a ground-shaking explosion of thunder.

Janna started shivering. "That was too close."

Michael nodded as he scanned their surroundings. "I think I'll just sit this one out."

There were several rocks the size of bean bags piled under the lee of the ledge. He waited until she sat, then settled onto the one next to her. When she shivered again, he draped an arm around her shoulders and pulled her close.

Thankful for the shared warmth, she snuggled a little closer. He smelled of fresh rain and a faint hint of aftershave, and she found herself wondering what it might be like to be kissed by him. She felt herself flush, and shifted slightly away so he wouldn't notice.

"Did you see anything unusual up on the trail?"

He chuckled, and she felt the deep vibration of it against her. "Besides the back end of my horse, who was heading east?"

"I promise, Mopsy and I will have a talk about that." She looked up at him, and saw his smile fade.

"I found the rock slide," he said somberly. "It's a miracle that you and your horse weren't swept off the trail. There's about twenty feet where it's now completely impassable."

She shivered again, and this time it wasn't from the cold.

"It just seemed odd that tons of rock would break free at the exact moment you were passing by. What are the chances? So I tied Mopsy to a tree and found another way up to the top, on foot."

She held her breath.

"I searched the area. The guy was careful. He didn't leave much of anything behind. But I did find evidence that someone must have been using a pickax near the ledge."

The implication was clear. "Someone was *waiting* there? Waiting for me?"

"That's my guess."

"Someone who knew I'd started riding up there every morning?"

"And probably spent considerable time choosing the best place, then started loosening those rocks. My guess is that he never thought his efforts would trigger that much of rock slide—but once some of them fell, the entire edge just gave way."

So someone had been following her on her lovely, quiet rides alone. And while she'd been savoring the solitude and magnificent scenery, he'd been analyzing where she went and he was planning what to do next.

But that stranger was no longer simply trying to scare her into closing the lodge.

He wanted to see her die.

Janna couldn't sleep.

Restless, she stared at the clock on the bedside table and groaned in frustration, willing away the dark images that had filled her thoughts since coming down off the mountain this evening.

The lodge and cabins had been her dream since the day her husband walked out despite her efforts to save their marriage.

Starting a new life here had seemed like a perfect answer to her heartfelt prayers. Yet nothing was turning out quite as she'd planned.

Tessa was still coolly distant. Claire's hostility had only increased, though that could signal the advancement of her Alzheimer's. Bringing the facility back to life was proving more complicated and expensive than she'd expected.

And now, her plan for creating this new life for Rylie and her at the lodge was placing them in danger.

God, did I misunderstand? Was this just a foolish dream, and not what I should have chosen? Am I stubbornly keeping us at risk by staying here?

If her stalker knew about her trail rides, he had to know about the deputy sheriff's presence here. Maybe that had provided a layer of protection against any outright confrontations. But what would happen when Michael and Ian moved to town?

Troubled, she pushed back her covers and paced her room, then slipped quietly down the hallway to the great room of the lodge.

A few glowing embers still pulsed in the fireplace, but the room was chilly, cast in eerie silver and black relief by the moonlight streaming through the expanse of windows facing west.

Shivering at the cold oak flooring beneath her

bare feet, she grabbed a Navajo blanket from the back of a sofa and wrapped herself in it, then added some pine twigs for kindling and a few lengths of hardwood to the fire.

The fire caught, crackling and snapping as it devoured the kindling, releasing the delicious, tangy scent of pine.

The growing flames sent golden light dancing into the room.

A chair creaked, and Janna looked up to find her mother sitting in one of the chairs back in the shadows, watching her. "Why don't you come closer to the fire?"

She didn't expect Claire to respond, much less follow her suggestion, and felt an absurd flash of pleasure when her mother rose and settled in a high, wing chair opposite hers.

The flickering light deepened the weathered lines and wrinkles in Claire's face, adding decades to her years. "You could tell me what's going on," she said after a long and stony silence. "I think it's only fair."

Janna considered and discarded a dozen breezy replies, buying time by crouching at the fireplace to rearrange the logs on the grate. She'd tried to avoid conveying her unease, knowing that Claire could do nothing to help and that her spells of dementia made her moods unpredictable at best.

What could she have overheard?

As if she'd read Janna's mind, Claire snorted. "I

might have been a lousy mother, but I've got eyes. You don't believe the damage to that cabin was random, for one thing. There were my flat tires, and something must have happened when you went riding today. You probably think it all has something to do with those bones. Or maybe, that it's all related to me."

Surprised, Janna looked over her shoulder. "You?"

"That should hardly be a surprise." Claire's voice turned bitter. "Especially to you. I know I've made enemies here—but I'd do it all over again to protect this ranch."

Their shared past loomed between them like fierce, roiling storm clouds—promising the end of their uneasy truce if either said another word.

The years of anger and impatience and criticism.

The complete inability to ever communicate.

The final, painful acceptance of the fact that her own mother was completely devoid of love and affection for her.

An empty chill spread through Janna as she eased back in her chair and pulled her blanket tighter around her shoulders. *There's no point in starting it all over again…just let it be. Please, just let it be.*

After a long silence she dragged her gaze from the fire and found Claire staring at her. "I no longer have the heart to argue, Mom."

Claire flinched at the affectionate term—one Janna had tried to quit using as a teenager, at Claire's stern request. "I was never much of a 'mom' to you.

We both know that, but you weren't much of a daughter, either."

If Claire had delivered a slap to Janna's face, it couldn't have been more painful. Janna stood and started for her bedroom. "Then I guess we were both failures."

"Wait!"

The command was worthy of any army general, but Janna knew she had to keep moving or risk saying words she could never take back.

"Please."

If Claire had ever uttered the word "please" in her life, Janna hadn't heard it. She stopped. "I'm not sure there's anything more we can say right now that won't be hurtful. It's probably better to just forget this whole conversation."

"Your father didn't die."

Stunned, Janna turned around. The room seemed to tip for a moment, and she had to reach out to brace herself against the back of a chair. *"What?"*

"Not exactly."

Claire's eyes took on a faraway look, as if she were retreating into the past, and Janna wondered if she were lost in some sort of delusion. The doctor had warned Janna and her sisters not to believe everything their mother said.

"You're either dead, or you're not," Janna said cautiously.

"Oh, now he is. Finally." Claire's voice hardened.

"After I inherited this place, he wanted to turn it into the biggest Angus ranch ever. We mortgaged everything to buy the right bloodlines. We build new barns, advertised. Then times got hard, and he turned mean. Drank. When I got pregnant with you, he took off like a scalded hound with everything we had left in the bank."

Understanding dawned, and with it, compassion. "I'm so sorry."

"He nearly destroyed *everything*. This ranch. My future. At nine months pregnant, I was herding cattle. I could afford no one else."

"That's something I can't change," Janna said quietly. "None of it was my choice."

"No, but you're a dreamer, just like him. Smart and stubborn and mouthy, and you always thought you were way too good for this ranch. I needed help—but you had your nose in your books. You only had to open your sassy mouth, and it always seemed like your daddy was still here—right in my face." Claire's chin lifted. "I figure you at least deserve to hear the truth."

Janna struggled with this first, clear glimpse of her father. A man who'd probably gone toe-to-toe with his wildly independent and dominant wife on a daily basis—not that it excused him for running away and taking the money she desperately needed.

It must have been the worst possible match.

"I always loved books, Momma. I dreamed of college from the time I was little. But I did help you out. I worked on this ranch a lot. I can't help that I wasn't a tomboy like Leigh and Tessa." Janna searched her mother's face for acceptance and found none. "Couldn't you have loved me for who I was—just a little?"

"Of course I did. I'm your mother." Claire stood, cinched the belt on her robe a little tighter and brushed past Janna on her way to the door. "Don't wake me up in the morning for breakfast. I think I'll sleep in."

Of course I did. I'm your mother. The cold tone certainly belied her words.

Janna stayed by the fireplace until dawn, watching the fire burn low, fade to embers and then finally flicker into cold, charred remnants.

Her mother's revelations bit deep.

Tessa and Leigh had both been through failed relationships but had never married, and Janna's own husband had left, just as her father had thirty years before. The McAllister legacy wasn't a happy one for finding deep and abiding love.

With every passing day she felt a deeper connection to Michael, and found herself looking forward to the moment he pulled up at his cabin after work, hoping there'd be a chance to talk with him.

But it would never lead to anything more, because she couldn't take that chance.

Carl had once seemed like the perfect man, too— before they were married. Then he'd immersed himself in his career with late hours and long weekends.

He'd drifted away from their church, and from Janna—and he'd broken Rylie's heart whenever he forgot another promise to her during that sad and difficult time.

Now he honored her scheduled visits and was trying harder to be a good father despite the responsibilities of a new wife with children of her own. But it could never again be the same as a whole and happy family for Rylie.

And the thought of remarrying to create that illusion just wasn't an option.

A loveless childhood, a failed marriage—what were the odds that Janna could ever really make a relationship work? Zip, if her mother, sisters and divorce were any clue, and it simply wasn't worth the risk to try.

Rylie would become attached to a stepdad, then face yet another loss. And Janna would never put her through that kind of heartache again.

FOURTEEN

They'd missed church last Sunday because Rylie's leg was still more comfortable if propped up on pillows, and she had trouble maneuvering her cast. Today Janna was determined to make it.

Claire had muttered something about going along. Then she'd refused to get ready this morning and hadn't even come out of her room—probably preferring to wait until Janna and Rylie left for town.

Janna had little doubt that Claire felt awkward and embarrassed over her revelations last night, though she'd probably never admit it, even to herself.

Rylie, bless her heart, had been happy to go, even though the Sunday school program was on summer hiatus until after Labor Day. Janna helped her out of the truck, then handed her the pair of crutches.

Immediately, a cluster of kids broke away from the small crowd standing by the front steps of the church. They formed an awed circle around her, asking about her cast. Pastor Lindsberg strolled over as well, followed by Janna's old friends Maria and Betsy.

"We heard on the scanner about the search party for Rylie," he said. "We also heard it being canceled, or I'm sure a lot of us would have been on our way out to help."

Janna smiled. Wade had said that the locals listened to their scanners these days, and apparently he was right. "Michael and his son found her. She was just up the trail a ways but hurt her ankle and couldn't make it back."

Maria frowned at Rylie. "If I'd known, I would have brought you supper or something. You should have called!"

Being back in this warm and welcoming environment at church could almost help Janna forget her other problems, at least for a while. "We managed."

The pastor clapped Janna on the shoulder. "I'd better go get ready inside. Wonderful to see you again."

Maria glanced around, then bent closer and lowered her voice. "Is everything all right out at your place?"

"Of course. I'm making good progress on the cabins, and we should be ready to start advertising soon. This past week I hired Lauren Young to help out part-time. She's doing great."

"I meant with your mother," Marie whispered. "My cousin saw her arguing with a deputy on the side of the road a couple weeks ago. He said she was positively livid."

"Someone had sabotaged her two front tires. But—" Janna hesitated "—she'd also started going out of town on the wrong highway."

Maria shrugged. "Maybe she was going somewhere else."

"I don't think so." Janna fingered the extra sets of vehicle keys that she'd dropped into her pocket on her way out the door this morning. "I try to keep an eye on her."

"There's some talk going around town. I'm not one to gossip, you understand." Betsy bit her lower lip. "But some people don't like the idea of that lodge opening up again. I overheard Lowell Haskins and Bobby Jay Miller myself, and I wouldn't want to meet either one of them in a dark alley. There are others, too."

Janna stilled. "Who?"

Maria and Betsy exchanged glances, then Maria nervously smoothed the collar of her blouse and looked away. "There was a table of people at the café," she said. "They were all saying how they hated seeing Claire McAllister make a success of something else. They seemed to hold quite a grudge against her, though I don't know why."

"But it's me, not my mother this time," Janna protested. "It's my business."

"A couple of them…um—" Betsy's cheeks flamed "—talked about financial problems and suspicious accidents out at Snow Canyon."

Marie made a face. "And about something fishy going on with the books. You know we don't believe a word of it. But why would anyone start rumors like that?"

"I wish I knew." Janna sighed. "Though now I understand why the local septic companies aren't returning my calls. And with just two of them around, I don't have much choice."

Betsy frowned. "My uncle Earl owns Kraemer Septic & Backhoe. He hasn't called you back?"

Janna managed a weak smile. "Not yet."

"He isn't one who pays any attention to gossip, but I do know he's gotten way behind since his partner retired." She hiked a thumb toward a balding, portly man talking to an elderly couple. "That's him. I'll introduce you after church."

The bells in the steeple started tolling, and everyone began moving toward the open front doors.

Maria winked. "Believe me, she'll have that man at your doorstep on Monday, apologizing for the delay. Our Betsy has turned into a force to be reckoned with in these parts!"

"It's my blackberry pie," Betsy clarified with a grin. "Prayer and a slice of that pie can work miracles—in that order."

It wasn't just Earl who appeared at the lodge on Monday morning. He arrived with a flat bed tractor, flatbed trailer and a backhoe, and was soon joined by a county inspector named Ken Weatherby.

They both walked the area around the upper cabins for a good hour with clipboards in hand. Measured and conferred, scratched their heads, then walked off the area again and did some more figuring.

Janna watched them for a while, then went to the lodge to check on Rylie and Claire. By the time she made it back up the hill, the inspector was climbing into his truck.

Both men were frowning.

She looked between them. "What's up?"

"The system up here is old—really old—and it conforms with few of the current regulations," Earl said. "We're going to start with an eight-foot profile hole to study soil type and depth, so we can check current or recent high-groundwater levels. Once we get that information, we'll go from there."

"That doesn't sound good."

Earl lifted a shoulder. "If it isn't done right, the system won't work for any length of time, and you could contaminate your water supplies."

"And if the groundwater levels aren't okay?"

"You're looking at an elevated leach bed. Possibly a pump, but you'd have to hire an engineer for that." He gave her a sympathetic smile. "More money."

The inspector nodded. "You've also got an infestation of noxious weeds back here—non-native plants."

"But it's essentially wilderness!"

"Noxious weeds, all the same. Gotta control them, or the fines can run fifty dollars a day. State law."

She suddenly felt faint. "A *day?*"

The man's bushy eyebrows drew together and his mouth tightened. "Earl has a carbon copy of my preliminary report. The county's weed-and-pest control people will be coming out, and they can show you what to do. They can loan you the right equipment and sell you chemicals at a discount. Fines start if you don't meet the deadline they set."

"Oh." She blinked and belatedly remembered to close her mouth. This, on top of everything else?

The man started up his truck and drove away, leaving her staring at Earl. "This has *not* been my day."

"Work has to be done, I'm afraid, unless you want to bulldoze these last four cabins. And you'll have to deal with those weeds no matter what. So, should I go ahead?"

Numbly she nodded and accepted the papers he handed her. She glanced through them with a feeling of doom. What in the world were diffuse knapweed, leafy spurge, or purple loosestrife? And exactly how hard would it be to get rid of them?

"I'd best get to work on that hole. If all goes well, I'll get your septic system done by the end of this week or next." He winked at her. "You got yourself one tough inspector, but don't you worry none about me. I'll be as fair as anyone in the county. I'd have to answer to my niece Betsy, otherwise."

"Weeds." Michael looked over the top rim of his sunglasses at her, then turned back to tightening the last screw on a door hinge in Cabin Three. "All that for weeds?"

Janna nodded glumly, obviously crestfallen as she watched the departure of an SUV emblazoned with the county's insignia. "The weed people figured it out per acre and type of herbicide. Even with using their equipment and buying discounted chemicals from the county, I'm looking at over five hundred dollars. Hiring professionals to do it would cost four times that. It isn't a choice, either. It's a state law, because these non-native weeds are apparently taking over habitat from the plants we do want."

Michael whistled.

"The inspectors will be back in a month to make sure I've complied." She brightened. "But the good news—the *really* good news today—was hearing about the septic field. The inspector evaluated the hole that Earl dug on Monday. We've got a green light, and it won't be nearly as expensive as Earl first thought. He'll start tomorrow, since his equipment is still here." She seemed to catch herself, then she laughed aloud. "Believe me, I never imagined myself quite this elated over a septic field."

For two years he'd nursed his wounds, struggling

with Elise's offhand dismissal of their marriage and her refusal to even discuss counseling or reconciliation. He'd always honored their marriage vows, even when she'd blithely ignored her own.

In the end, her death had driven home the point more painfully than anything else. He'd failed her, and he'd failed himself. Since then, the thought of ever attempting another relationship had made his blood run cold. Until now.

The time he'd spent here at Snow Canyon Lodge had slowly changed that. Inexorably. He'd watched Janna face challenges and not give up, watched her loving care of her daughter and her patience with the irascible woman who was her mother, though he had yet to see the old woman show the slightest hint of affection in return.

And now, despite the fact that she was facing even more problems, there was a sparkle of joy in her eyes that completely captured his heart. He grinned at her, feeling as if his world had taken a dizzying spin in a new direction, to a place where happiness might just be a possibility.

"Feel like celebrating?" he teased.

"Absolutely." She thought for a minute, then rested the fingertips of one hand at her throat. "Wow! I could go start on Cabin Nine!"

"Or maybe we could go out to dinner." He held his breath, unaware that he'd done so until she finally looked up and their eyes met.

"I…"

His heart skipped a beat.

"I…I would like that, Michael." A faint blush stained her cheeks. "Very much. But I can't leave Rylie and my mother here alone, and Lauren isn't here today. I'm so sorry."

"Ian could stay with them."

She wavered, searching his face. "I could try calling Lauren. I'm not sure Ian would like playing babysitter."

"He's seventeen, so he could handle things for a few hours. Especially if I paid him."

She hesitated only a moment longer. "Okay, but only if we aren't late. Eight or nine? With everything that's happened here…"

He smiled. "The steak house is just on the other side of town. I'll have you back in a couple of hours—well before dark. Deal?"

"Deal." She glanced down at her muddied shorts and old tennis shoes and cried out in dismay. "Give me twenty minutes, or the manager of that place won't even let me in."

Michael's amusement faded as he watched her jog toward the lodge, her pretty blond hair swinging with every step.

He'd courted his late wife with plays. The symphony. Quiet candlelit dinners and strolls on the beach. Intelligent and charming, Elise had always loved dressing in pearls and high heels, with flirty little black dresses that showed off her pretty figure. She'd even agreed to start going to church with him—for a while, anyway, before she'd found herself too busy.

A perfect woman, a perfect courtship.

He'd done everything he could to please her, yet it had never been enough. Their marriage had ended up like dust beneath his feet.

Maybe this time, he could get it right.

But even as he headed back to his cabin to change clothes, his uncertainty grew.

Ian walked into the lodge, a portfolio under his arm, and found Rylie in the dining room, a five-hundred-piece puzzle spread out on one of the tables, her crutches leaning against the wall behind her.

He'd first started stopping by out of guilt for what had happened when he'd left her behind up on the trail. After that, he'd just kept dropping in because he felt sorry for her. It had to be awful, being cooped up in the lodge without much to do.

Now he could almost imagine her as a little sister, with her giggles and smiles, and her obvious adoration of him when he coached her on her drawing or took the time to play a few board games with her. Spiders frightened her, and he'd apparently even risen to hero status yesterday, after escorting a couple of big ones outside.

"I saw your mom and my dad on the porch," he said. "I guess they're going out for a steak or something. I think they're celebrating about a sewer." He rolled his eyes. "Sounds gross to me."

She grinned from ear to ear. "Me, too. Mom left macaroni and cheese and chocolate cake, if you'd like some. Those are my favorites."

He warily glanced around the room. "What about your grandma?"

"She didn't want to go to town. She already ate and now she's probably reading in her room. She doesn't like to come out here much."

Rylie led the way into the kitchen at a good clip, swinging along on her crutches. Ian helped her pull a casserole dish of macaroni and cheese out of the oven.

They'd just settled down to platefuls of it at a small table in the kitchen when a cheery voice shouted out a hello. *Lauren?*

Ian's heart fell to someplace in the vicinity of his ankles. Great. The perky Miss Young had just turned up. Just what he needed.

He'd avoided her for a whole week, still embarrassed over the day she'd seen all of his ugly scars and had turned away in disgust.

He took a self-conscious glance at his clothes—a hoodie sweatshirt and jeans—then snorted at himself. Why should he care what anyone thought?

Rylie called out to Lauren and she popped into the kitchen a second later, smiling happily until her eyes settled on Ian, then skated away. She faltered to a stop. "There was a call—on our answering machine. I thought—"

"Mom didn't hear back, so she asked Ian," Rylie chirped. "But that's cool. Now we can all play Monopoly or something!"

"Um, I don't think so." High color bloomed in her cheeks. "I should probably just go."

Memories of the not-too-subtle stares at high school flooded into Ian's thoughts. All of the humiliation, the self-consciousness, knowing that people were always talking behind his back, as if he were deaf as well as scarred. Mocking him.

"Yeah, right, it's pretty creepy being in the same room with a guy like me." The words escaped before he could even think.

Rylie sucked in a sharp breath.

Lauren's mouth fell open. *"What?"*

He knew he should stop, but he just couldn't hold back the bitter words that kept coming. "You think I don't know what you thought? That I don't hear what people say?"

"Ian," Rylie said, her face stricken.

The note of fear in her voice hit him like a bucket of ice water. He ducked his head in apology. "Sorry. Look, you two just do—whatever. I'll go back to my cabin and read."

Lauren's delicate brows drew together. "I…I don't know what that was all about, but it was sorta scary. Are you all right? I mean, you're the one who snubbed *me*, bucko."

He drew back. "What?"

She looked almost angry. "You don't think *I* know how it is?" When he didn't answer, she made a slicing motion with her hand. "The rich kids do that all the time, and I'm sick of it. I'm just glad to be done with high school, I'll tell you."

"Rich kids?"

Her gaze dropped to the floor, but then her chin came up and her eyes flashed with defiance. "My dad's a drunk, and my mom left this year. But that doesn't change who *I* am."

She looked like some teen superstar, with her long, shiny black hair and pretty face. She had no idea how bad things could be, but the thought of someone like her facing her own struggles stunned him. He took a deep breath. "I thought you saw my scars and were grossed out."

"What scars?" Her eyes settled on his wrist, where the tail end of one showed. "You oughta see my brother Rex. He rodeos, and he is *so* not good at it. Spends more time getting stitches than he does riding broncs." Her mouth twitching, she lifted her gaze to meet Ian's. "I thought you were just some snotty rich kid, looking down on the hired help."

Rylie heaved an overly dramatic sigh of relief. "Since we can all be friends, now, how about that game of Monopoly?"

"Sure, kid. That would be fun." Lauren peered around her. "What's that?"

Before Ian could react, Rylie slid off her chair and

reached for the portfolio. "Ian helps me with my drawing, and he promised to bring me some of his pictures tonight."

Embarrassed, he wanted to grab the folder and run with it before either of them looked at his awkward attempts. But he swallowed hard and watched as Lauren opened it and studied the first drawing—a pencil sketch he'd done of the chipmunks that spent the day scampering around just outside his cabin.

"I, uh, that was the first one I kept," he managed in a strangled voice. "I know it's rough."

"Wow. That's good!" Rylie said, looking over at him with admiration shining in her eyes. Then she turned back to Lauren. "He had an awful accident, and he can't use his hand very well anymore. So we're learning together."

The two girls reverently lifted one page after another, studying each one…and then lingered over the last one. Belatedly, he remembered it was a drawing he'd done of Rylie and Lauren one night when he couldn't sleep. He felt his face heat up.

"Wow," Rylie breathed. "I didn't know you drew us!"

Lauren touched a fingertip to the sketch he'd done of her and stared at it for a long, agonizing moment. He imagined her being angry, or creeped out…or just a little too patronizing.

But when she finally looked up at him, there was

a sheen of tears in her eyes. "I...I don't know what to say."

She was so upset that she was gonna *cry?* Alarm raced through him. "I'm sorry. Really, I—"

She shook her head and smiled at him through her tears. "No, no—this just blows me away. No one has ever done something like this for me. Ever. Is there any way...could you let me have it?"

Absurdly pleased, he nodded.

Rylie grinned. "Good. So how about Monopoly?"

Lauren set up the game on a table in the dining room, while Ian made sure all the doors and windows were locked at her request. "Babysitter rules," she said with a grin.

They'd all made it around the board and passed Go twice when Maggie stirred from her usual place by the fireplace and trotted in to see them, then put her paws up on a low windowsill to peer out.

Maggie growled—something Ian always thought was just too funny, coming from something that looked like a dirty dust mop.

"Your turn, Ian," Rylie prodded. "Roll the dice!"

The dog growled again, louder this time, and they all turned to look out the window. The sun was low in the sky, sending long shadows across the grass, but nothing was stirring out there.

Dumb dog—probably just heard a squirrel.

He reached for the dice...but then he heard

something, too. A single, metallic clank coming from far away.

They all stilled, glancing at each other.

But there was only silence now, but for the lonely hoot of a distant owl.

"Maybe it's just the wind," Lauren finally ventured. "Or one of the horses knocking over a pail."

Ian nodded, relieved at the logical explanation and thankful that he hadn't reacted with fear. That would have been *sooo* lame in front of a nine-year-old and a cool girl like Lauren.

Still, he kept listening, and when the girls were focused on the game board, he kept glancing outside.

What if Lauren was wrong?

FIFTEEN

Janna smiled as she looked around the rustic steak house. "I love all the pine," she murmured, toying with the salad fork at the side of her plate. "And the aromas from that kitchen are out of this world."

Michael nodded and went back to studying the menu.

Fresh trout. Prime rib. Shrimp scampi. Filet mignon. Familiar fare for an upscale steak house, but surprising at this small one tucked away in Wolf Creek, Wyoming. The plates passing by on the lone waiter's arm were all beautifully prepared.

But none of it sounded good tonight.

"You don't look happy, though," she said quietly. "Do you want to go somewhere else?"

He looked up and found her smiling at him.

"I did change my clothes, honest," she added with a twinkle in her eye. "*And* I took a shower."

"It isn't you."

She rolled her eyes. "The old *Seinfeld* line,

right? 'It isn't you—it's me' as a way to escape a bad date?"

He felt a twinge of guilt. "Any guy in town would be lucky to be here with you."

"Except you."

The last thing he'd ever wanted to do was hurt her feelings, yet now it was probably inevitable. "I'm just not good company right now."

Her expression softened. "I know you've had hard times in the past. Losing you wife…dealing with your son. We're friends, right? No expectations—just two grown-ups, out for a nice meal. Nothing more."

He'd wanted more this afternoon. More time to get to know her, to see where this relationship could lead. More time to enjoy conversation and her laughter. He'd seen that same interest in her eyes when he'd asked her to dinner.

Then he'd realized that he just wasn't ready. After ruining so many lives, he probably never would be. "I'm sorry."

Her hesitation lasted only an instant, and then she rallied. "Hey, I'm just happy to have a few hours away from the lodge. So, what looks good on the menu?"

He scanned the menu again and chose quickly when the waiter approached to take their order.

"See, that wasn't so hard," she teased, then leaned forward and lowered her voice. "So, tell me—have you heard anything from the DCI?"

"I called yesterday, but they won't even start on

this case for a good long while. They did tell me that the bones were from a middle-aged male, but that's about it."

"Anything else?"

"Knowing the approximate age and sex of the deceased weeded out the only missing persons reports I found for the time frame we're looking at."

She shuddered. "What were the others?"

"A couple of women. A child—though that was considered a parental abduction because the noncustodial parent fled to his native Mexico."

"And the women just disappeared?"

"One was a college girl from Montana who was backpacking alone somewhere in this part of the Rockies. The other was in her early thirties, and in an abusive marriage. Her husband was actually sentenced to life based on circumstantial evidence and a long history of 911 calls by his wife, though her body was never found."

Their Caesar salads arrived, along with a warm, fragrant miniloaf of pumpernickel on a wooden cutting board.

She lifted a forkful of lettuce, then paused. "What about the coyote that was left in the cabin?"

He eyed her salad. "You're sure you want to talk about this now?"

She nodded.

"The vet recovered the kind of slug from the carcass that shows the shooter buys ammo for big game, not varmints. And he must've been a good distance away when he took aim, or the slug would have gone right through."

"So he's a good shot." She shivered. "Can you tell what kind of rifle it was?"

"Hundreds of models could take that ammo size. For ballistics reports you need the rifle for comparison."

Her shoulders slumped in defeat. "So we're still at a dead end."

"Not entirely—thanks to the rock slide."

"You can analyze *rocks?*"

"Cigarettes." He smiled. "I found one wedged deep between some rocks at the top of the cliff—and it clearly hadn't been there very long. So I did some checking, and Catabrese Golds aren't sold anywhere west of the Mississippi, except by mail order or online. Perhaps the buyer can be traced."

"A lucky break, then…unless it belonged to some hiker."

"It's now on the way to the DCI for analysis and should yield saliva DNA and fingerprints. If the person has a record, we could be very close to nailing him."

Janna's smile lit up her face. "What a relief that'll be!"

"In the meantime, I don't want you or the kids outside after dusk, and you need to be very, very careful. Promise?"

"Of course."

He hesitated. "The work on my house in town has been completed faster than anticipated. I need to start spending more time there so I can get the rest of the work done."

"I understand completely." Janna looked away. "You can forget about that contract holding you to the entire summer."

"No, I'll still be at the cabin at night, just not during the evenings."

"You really don't need to—"

"Yes, I do. At least until we find out who has been causing trouble out there." He put down his fork. "Honestly, I'd feel a lot better if you and your family got a few rooms at the motel in town—at least until this is over. You could run out to the lodge during the day, if need be."

"My mother would never agree to letting some jerk run us off our property," she retorted. "And for once, I'm on her side."

The next morning Janna heard the sound of a pickup rumbling up the hill while she was working in Cabin Nine. She hurried out the front door and waved, then went outside as soon as she finished scrubbing out the kitchen cupboards.

She found Earl standing by the backhoe, arguing into the cell phone at his ear. "That isn't soon enough," he barked.

He jerked the phone from his ear, punched in

another number and started another terse conversation before noticing that she'd joined him.

Disappointed at what she was hearing, she stared at the gaping hole he'd dug at the beginning of the week.

He muttered something into the phone, then jammed it in the breast pocket of his work shirt. "Out of luck, ma'am. Leastways, for now."

"It's really *broken?* You're kidding!"

Fuming, he rounded the front of the machine and pointed. "See there, on the backhoe boom? The metal hydraulic line has a crack in it, and the fluid is gone. I think the fuel pump is shot, too." Earl shoved his ball cap back and scratched his head. "This rig hasn't given me a lick of trouble all year. It ran like a top on Monday."

She mentally counted up the remaining weeks of the tourist season and said a silent prayer. "But you can fix it, right?"

"Sure, once I get the parts." He slapped his cap against his thigh. "But it ain't easy to get 'em for this old gal. No one in Jackson has what it needs, so I'll have to order from a shop down in Denver. That takes time."

"Any idea how long it might take?"

"A week, maybe two. Once it took over a month."

"A *month!*"

He shrugged and started for his pickup. "It shouldn't take that long. I'll do what I can."

"One last thing—" she hesitated "—you mentioned that it's been running fine. It seems strange that two things suddenly went wrong."

"I take good care of my equipment, if that's what you're getting at. Breakdowns happen."

"You think someone could've tampered with it?"

He snorted. "Who would come clear out here, when this rig is usually parked right behind my house? Makes no sense to me."

His eyes narrowed as he went back to the machine and took a closer look at the fuel pump, then ran a hand along the metal hydraulic line. He paused and bent over for a close look at the underside. "I don't recollect a dent there. And once I pull that fuel pump, I'm going to take a mighty close look."

Janna watched him drag his tools out of the back of his pickup and start dismantling the backhoe, then she went back to work in the cabin, her heart heavy.

Just this morning she'd awakened early to work on the Snow Canyon Lodge Web site, adding photos and descriptions of the cabins that were ready, and posting the rates and dates available.

She'd anticipated a small but growing trickle of e-mails in response, because most of the resorts in the area filled up months ahead of the season. Newly available rentals could spur considerable interest—she hoped.

But now, the four farthest cabins would remain out of commission for weeks or even longer by the time the backhoe was repaired, the septic system finished and the inspectors arrived.

She shuddered at the thought of her anemic bank account, and the effect of missing so much of the tourist season. She'd started with a small inheritance from Uncle Gray, and a much smaller amount of money in her savings. What would happen when that ran out? The money was going fast—for repairs and updates, rustic cabin furnishings, kitchenware and linens.

It wasn't just the worry about someone trying to make her fail. It could be sheer economics that made it happen.

And last night…

She'd wavered between relief, sadness and disbelief at the conversation she and Michael had shared at the steak house, when he'd practically echoed the very things *she'd* planned to say.

The irony of that awkward conversation had been running through her mind ever since.

He was a wonderful man. She'd come to care for him way too much. But, like him, she knew there was no place in her life for another relationship. After the sad, slow death of a marriage she'd tried so hard to save, the idea of risking another failure was just too overwhelming to contemplate…and there just wasn't enough joy and hope left in her heart to try.

So why did she still feel such an empty place in her heart after hearing Michael say he felt the same way?

Uneven footsteps, punctuated by the thumps of

crutches, came up the steps and across the porch. "Mom!"

"What's up?" Janna rose slowly, working the stiffness out of her back, and opened the screen door wide. "Oh, Rylie—what have you been into?"

The child's cast was muddy, as were her clothes and hands. "I—I went for a walk. I wanted to see the big hole before it was gone." Rylie held out her hand. "There were some old dishes and stuff in that big pile of dirt. And look what I found! You can have it, 'cause it doesn't fit me."

Inwardly cringing at the contamination that might be in the soil, Janna gingerly accepted what looked like a small ball of mud, and rubbed at it with a forefinger. "What is it?"

"It's an old ring, but it doesn't have diamonds or anything. Maybe it's part of a secret treasure or something. I'm going back to look—"

"No, you're not, young lady." Janna dropped the muddy object on the kitchen table that she'd temporarily set out on the porch. "You could fall in that hole, and you could get hurt again. We're going right up to the house and get you in the bathtub. *Now.* Aunt Tessa said she'd come for you and your grandma at two o'clock, and you need to be ready."

Managing a garbage-sack wrapping of the cast during Rylie's bath, helping her dress and also trying to scrub the cast itself took the better part of an hour.

By the time Rylie was ready, Claire had been pacing the lodge for twenty minutes, and Tessa had been waiting for ten.

"Sorry," Janna said as she ushered her daughter into the lobby. "Rylie did some unexpected exploring, and she had to get cleaned up."

Claire, apparently in a good mood because she was going back to the ranch overnight, eyed her granddaughter with interest. "So, what did you find?"

"Cool stuff," Rylie exclaimed. "Up in the big dirt pile. Some old spoons and dishes and even—"

"Please." Tessa raised a brow at Janna. "Not where they're digging up the old septic lines. Tell me you didn't let her play there."

Janna silently counted to ten. "She went up there on her own, I'm afraid. Her first solo excursion out of the lodge since she got her cast on."

"Leastways she shows a little spunk," Claire sniffed.

Rylie looked up at her grandmother in surprise, clearly warming to the rare compliment.

With an expression of distaste, Tessa glanced out the window toward the only cabins visible from the lodge. "I suppose you were busy with one of those awful cabins at the time. Beats me why anyone would want to stay clear out here."

"You'd be surprised. I checked my e-mail a few minutes ago and found three reservations for next month."

"Three!" Claire appeared taken aback. "But where on earth will you put them all?"

"We'll have plenty of room by then," Janna assured her. "Michael and Ian have been helping with some repairs, and I've been making good progress, too."

"Can we go?" Rylie vibrated with excitement as she looked between the adults. "I'm all ready—pajamas and everything!"

They all trooped out to Tessa's crew-cab pickup, where Janna put Rylie's overnight bag in the back, gave her a big hug and then helped her into the back seat. "I'll miss you, sweetie," Janna murmured. "Be a good girl for Aunt Tessa, okay? No exploring?"

"Promise." Rylie looked down at Janna's hand. "You didn't like my present?"

"Present?"

Rylie raised her hurt gaze to meet Janna's. "The ring."

"Oh, my—of course I did. I'll get it right now and clean it up. Then maybe we can share it, okay?"

Janna waved as the truck disappeared down the lane.

Michael was at work. Ian was somewhere on the property—probably with his nose in a book. Lauren was cleaning in one of the cabins. Still, with Rylie and Claire gone, the place suddenly seemed terribly quiet.

Tonight would be even worse, staying alone in the cavernous lodge without Rylie's chatter and Claire's acerbic comments to fill the silence.

Not that there weren't a thousand things to fill her time. But before anything else, she needed to retrieve that trinket from Cabin Nine, or Rylie would be even more disappointed.

She jogged up the hill and met Lauren and Ian who were coming down, side by side. She hid a smile at their budding friendship. "What's up?"

"Ian's dad wants him to choose the colors for his room at the house in town before the hardware store closes. Is it all right if I take him? I'm nearly done for today, anyhow."

"Not a problem. Afterward, maybe you can even have some fun—go inner tubing on one of the creeks, or go to Tessa's and sign up for a trail ride. Just be sure to let Ian's dad know."

"Thanks!" The two broke into a run and raced down the hill, Ian's limp far less obvious than it had been before. His tough shell of defiance had faded, and yesterday, he'd even joined them all in a meal-time prayer.

Progress, she thought. *In so many ways. Thank you, Lord, for how you take care of your children.*

She found the mud-caked object where she'd left it earlier. A faint, dull bit of gold color showed through the dirt, and she smiled at Rylie's "treasure."

It was probably a child's piece of cheap, dime-store jewelry. Something out of a gumball machine. But to Rylie, it would always be special because she'd come across it in such an exciting way.

Gingerly picking it up, Janna took it back to the lodge and dropped it into a bowl of hot, sudsy water.

But when she withdrew it a half hour later, she blinked.

Held it up to the light. Grabbed a terry cloth dish towel and vigorously polished it, then stared at it again.

Possibilities raced through her thoughts at what Rylie had found…in dirt that had been excavated not more than 100 yards from where Maggie had found the bones.

It was a woman's ring.

A college ring, in heavy gold with intricate scroll-work and an incredible opal with dazzling fire. The kind of ring that had probably cost the earth, and it had come from an expensive private college out East.

It was the kind of ring that one would search for endlessly until it was found.

So what was it doing in a pile of excavated dirt? The most likely scenario was that someone simply lost it, but an uneasy chill of foreboding swept through Janna all the same.

The delicate script on the side said 1990. The approximate year of the murder.

What if its owner had come here—and never left?

SIXTEEN

Janna moved to a sunny window in the kitchen and held the ring up to the light once more. It was the loveliest class ring she'd ever seen. A wave of unspeakable sadness swept through her over the secrets it might hold.

She left a message on Michael's cell phone, then called the sheriff's office. The secretary said he was helping the highway patrol with a major accident outside of Salt Creek and might not be back for another hour.

He planned to paint some rooms in his house tonight, so Janna might not even see him until tomorrow.

But since the moment she'd seen the ring, a small, insistent voice in her head had started a litany that would not stop. *Don't wait....don't wait...*

Frowning, she glanced at the late-afternoon shadows lengthening across the yard. The hair at her nape prickled. *Foolishness,* she admonished herself.

Yet…if she went to town, she might see Michael sooner, and she could certainly use a run to the grocery store for more supplies. If she made it in time, she could even pick up her limited-liability document at the lawyer's office, so it could be framed and posted at the lobby registration desk.

She pocketed the ring, grabbed her purse and locked up the lodge, but out on the porch she hesitated, then withdrew the ring and tried it on several fingers until she found a perfect fit. "I don't want to lose you," she murmured.

With a last glance at her watch, she hurried to her truck.

Connie, the pretty secretary in the sheriff's office, had been a few years ahead of Janna in school. She smiled in welcome when Janna walked through the door.

But she shook her head when Janna asked if Michael was on his way back. "Fatalities," she said grimly. "And there's a chemical spill all over the highway. The environmental people aren't even there yet."

"Can I leave him a message?" When Connie handed her a pad of phone message forms, Janna wrote a quick note about finding something that might be evidence and passed it back. "It's not an emergency. I'd just like to talk to him today if possible. Have you seen his son recently?"

"He met his dad here just before that 911 call came in. I believe he and Lauren Young arranged to go out to your sister's place for some sort of a moonlight trail ride and cook-out."

"Sounds like fun." She glanced up at the clock on the wall. The law office would be closing in five minutes, the grocery store in a half hour. "Oops, I'd better run. Thanks!"

She crossed the street and hurried several doors down. The sign in the large plate glass window of the law office said Closed, but she could see Wade standing behind the open blinds, reaching for the cord to shut them.

She waved and made a pleading gesture with her hands. He motioned her toward the front door, unlocked it and ushered her in.

"I saw you headed this way and thought I'd better wait." He gave her a benevolent, gentle smile. "Your liability statement, right? It's on my desk."

She followed him back to his office, where he settled into his chair and sifted through a stack of papers. He handed over the document, with an invoice paper clipped to it.

But when she accepted it, his gaze fell on her hand, and he gave a low whistle. "That's quite an opal," he marveled. He took her hand and drew it farther over his desk to admire the stone. "So much fire. My mother adores them, so I'm afraid I ended up quite the connoisseur." Again, the soft, almost obsequious smile. "I don't suppose you'd consider parting with this one? For a fair price, of course. I could have it reset for her."

"Probably not. But I'll certainly let you know if I ever do." Uncomfortable with the awkward position of her arm, Janna withdrew her hand and pulled her checkbook out of her purse.

He shook his head. "Please, don't bother right now. You've got thirty days, and I've already closed out my books for the day."

Surprised and grateful, she rose. "By then I'll have regular cabin guests arriving, so that will be perfect. Thanks!"

He walked her to the door and opened it for her. "So things are going well?"

"Very. Almost on schedule, too."

"Almost?"

"We still need to correct the septic problems, and Earl's backhoe broke down."

He shook his head. "Good luck. I sit on the county board and have coffee with some of the county guys every Monday morning. I've heard that some of Earl's clients had to hire someone else after he botched things up and couldn't get past the inspections. Cost those people a ton of money for the work and the legal fees."

Janna felt her heart sink. "He seems like a nice man."

"But he could end up costing far more than you expected, and that's a fact. The question is—just how deep in debt do you want to go with that place?"

The question rankled, but she forced a breezy smile and turned for the door. "Whatever it takes, I guess."

"Well, I'd just be careful, if I were you." He rested a hand on her shoulder. "And not just with that money pit."

She froze, halfway out the entrance. "Why?"

"There's just some talk, you understand. But it had to start somewhere." He looked over her shoulder at the empty sidewalk before continuing. "My housekeeper's son is a wild one, and he told her about some guy out at the Hilltop Tavern last weekend. Drunk as a skunk, bragging about how the McAllisters were going to be sorry they ever messed with him."

Lowell Haskins? Or the shadowy figure she'd seen in the woods a month ago? They could even be one and the same, which would make perfect sense. Janna's stomach tightened. "Did you hear his name?"

"No, but it sounds like he was either an employee or did business with your family." Wade's brows knit together in a worried frown. "I still worry about you living out in the middle of nowhere, with someone like Lowell on the area. I saw him in front of the tavern not an hour ago, so be careful."

"I will." She smiled and patted his arm on her way out, thankful for his concern. "I do know my way around a shotgun, and definitely won't hesitate to use it."

* * *

Janna hesitated in front of the grocery store, then turned on her heel and sauntered down toward the tavern. Sure enough, Lowell was lounging in front with a couple of other cowboys, a cigarette dangling from his lips.

He blew out a cloud of smoke and eyed her, his mouth twisted in a sneer. "If it isn't a McAllister. We should be honored."

The other two laughed, then vanished into the tavern, leaving her face-to-face with a man who clearly despised her simply for who she was. *Please, God, help me find the right words. I don't want to make things worse.*

He drew deeply on his cigarette, then dropped it to the sidewalk and ground it into the cement with the heel of his boot.

She eyed the cigarette, wanting to grab it for evidence. Wondering how she could manage without being too obvious.

He followed her gaze, then picked it up himself and, fixing a cold stare on her face, rolled it between his fingers until it crumbled to shreds of tobacco. "Cat got your tongue?"

"I—I'm just trying to understand." She lifted her chin. "I don't know even know you, yet this is the second time you've been rude. And now I hear around town that you've been threatening us."

"Have I?" He shrugged. He pulled a near-empty

pack of cigarettes out of his shirt pocket and shook one out, his palm covering the brand name on the package. "Now, what could an old, broke cowboy like me do to the likes of you? And why would I care?"

He lit the cigarette.

Dropped the match.

Then touched the brim of his hat in a mocking gesture. "See you around, Ms. McAllister. I'm just real sure I'll see you around."

During her fast trip through the grocery store, Janna sorted through the possibilities.

It had been weeks since she'd seen anyone lurking out in the woods, but the problems at the lodge had been escalating. Slowly. Inexorably.

Just how far would this enemy go, and what was the culprit after?

Given the speed of small-town gossip, everyone in town knew about the bones by now, and knew it could be a year or more before there were answers. Plenty of time for a killer to pack up and leave town if he feared that the DCI might find some sort of identifying evidence.

So, if Lowell—or someone else—had anything to do with the murder, why wouldn't he or she flee to some distant state?

Janna stowed her groceries in the back of her pickup and drove to the edge of town. She eyed the cheerful sign for a small B&B, and for the first time she hesitated about going home. Everyone was gone. She'd be alone until Michael and Ian returned to their cabin late tonight. If the painting project took longer than expected, maybe Michael would even call Ian and have him come back into town after the trail ride, rather than risk driving the narrow mountain roads leading up to the lodge.

But there was also the possibility that Lauren could drop Ian back at the cabins, and then he would be there alone.

Janna had to go back.

Throwing the truck into gear, she drove through the low, flat floor of the valley, then turned up the gravel county road leading to Snow Canyon. The sun disappeared behind a heavy bank of clouds and the air grew ominously still. Not a blade of grass moved.

Then the sky turned to indigo and a stiff wind came up, pelting the side of the truck with rain and swirls of gravel.

She hunched forward to make out the road ahead between swipes of the wipers that couldn't keep up with the deluge. She debated about pulling over, but the road was narrow, and vehicles coming in either direction might mistake her for a moving vehicle and plow right into her.

Several times she caught a glimpse of distant headlights in her rearview mirror, so it was a possibility.

The road wound higher and higher up the side of the mountain. From a single, clear vantage point on a hairpin turn she could see a dark vehicle, il-luminated for just a heartbeat by the flash of light-ning.

Odd. She was driving at a snail's pace. Most locals drove like they were on a speedway despite the dan-gerous roads, but this car was keeping a steady distance behind her. A vacationer, maybe, frightened by the terrain and the weather. Or…

She came around another bend in clear view of the road below and stopped. The other vehicle went slower, then eased to a halt, as well. Was he *following* her?

Wade's warnings ran through her brain, faster and faster. There were sheer drop-offs along this section of road. A thousand feet. Fifteen hundred feet or more. They led down to rocky, brush-strewn creek beds. Piles of boulders. Stands of pine and birch. Years ago a traveler had disappeared up here one autumn, and his car—with him in it—hadn't been found until spring melt.

If someone wanted retribution against the Mc-Allisters, this would be a perfect place to run a car off the road.

Her pulse raced as she stepped on the gas, easing along faster. The truck fishtailed precariously close to the edge on the next rain-slickened curve, sending her heart rocketing into her throat.

She eased up on the accelerator, breathless and shaking. Afraid to risk looking back again.

Five curving miles ahead, the road snaked down

into a valley before rising again, and there she would have cell-phone reception.

Halfway up that next hill was the turnoff to the lodge—where she had weapons locked away. *If I can just get there, Lord, I'll be safe. Please help me….*

Gripping the steering wheel even tighter, she blinked at the pouring rain. Maybe it was all just her imagination. The stuff of suspense movies. But when she began the descent into the valley, those headlights were still behind her.

Now they were *closer,* looming larger in her rearview mirror like some predatory animal, stalking its prey. *It's just my imagination. It's just my imagination. Surely nothing more than that.*

But even when the road flattened out, offering a good four-mile stretch of straight road and clear vision, the car behind her made no move to pass.

Her hand trembling, she speed-dialed Michael. No answer. She took a steadying breath. Left a voice message.

Then she punched in 911, but the signal faded while she was giving her name location. Dropping the phone into her lap in frustration, she gripped the steering wheel with both hands just in time to negotiate the first of the hairpin turns leading up out of the valley. The other car was with in thirty feet of her bumper.

Twenty.

Fifteen.

Like a mountain lion tensed and waiting for the perfect moment to attack.

She barely slowed for the entrance to the lodge grounds, but here she surely had an advantage. She knew each curve, each slope.

She accelerated, the wheels slipping on the wet gravel, taking the first curves like a race driver. Then she floored the accelerator for the straight run up to the lodge, where she circled behind the building, threw the truck into park and took off running, the door key ready in her fist.

Her leather-soled boots slipped and slid on the wet grass, and she nearly went down, then struggled to her feet and kept going, half running, half falling. *The rifles are inside. I've got to get to the rifles.*

Her lungs burning and muscles screaming, Janna closed the distance to the back door and nearly collapsed against it, fumbling frantically with the key—

A viselike grip encircled her from behind and lifted her off her feet. She kicked and fought, trying to reach behind to claw at her attacker. She sank her teeth into the hairy forearm clamped across her collarbones.

Her assailant grunted and tightened his grip until she could no longer breathe—then slammed her to the ground. She tried to scramble away, but the pouring rain obscured her vision, and her wet, muddy hair hung in front of her face like a dark curtain.

He caught her arm in a vicious grip that instantly

turned her hand numb, then jerked her around, and shook her until her head snapped back.

From somewhere in the distance…foggy, indistinct, came the low, venomous growl of an all-too familiar voice.

"You just wouldn't take a hint. You were too stupid to listen. So now, sweetheart, you're going to die."

SEVENTEEN

In a heartbeat, she knew who it was—though she could scarcely believe it. *Wade?*

Stunned, she tried to get a good look at him as he wrenched her to her feet and dragged her toward the trees, his long black Aussie oilskin coat flapping at his ankles.

A bolt of lightning sizzled through the air, and a sharp crack shook the earth. The stench of ozone and burning pine sap filled the air in an instant.

He flinched and swore under his breath, his grip loosening for a split second.

"Please…let me go!" she screamed over the wind and the rain, struggling to escape his grasp. But here the wet pine needles were ice-slick. She stumbled, then fell, unable to gain any leverage against him.

She grabbed for a pine tree, but the rough bark scraped her palm and wrist as he relentlessly hauled her forward until he reached Cabin Two.

There, he shoved her face-first into the outer wall,

wrenching her hands behind her back to loop a thin cord around her wrists. She flexed her wrists and fought to keep them separated, but he cinched the cord tight and then spun her around.

Disbelief turned her muscles to rubber. "Why? Wade—this is crazy!"

Panting heavily from exertion, his face red, Wade gave a single, harsh laugh, then his mouth twisted into a snarl. "You just couldn't take a hint. You could have closed this place up. Let it crumble to dust. But you couldn't leave it alone. Now, sweetheart, you have to join the others or my life will be in ruins."

She sucked in a sharp breath against the black spots dancing in front of her eyes. *"Others?"*

Once again he grabbed her arm, and now he shoved her up the steps and across the narrow porch, then kicked in the door. His voice turned smug. "The bones you found don't matter—I found that grave again years ago, and made sure there was no evidence left. Your friends at the DCI will never be able to identify him."

"'Don't matter'? How could a death not matter?" She tried to brace her feet against the door frame, but he wrestled her inside and threw her against the opposite wall.

Unable to catch her fall, Janna hit her head hard against the pine logs. A protruding nail stabbed her upper arm, ripping her shirt and her flesh as she crumpled into the corner. Searing pain snaked through her and hot, sticky blood dripped past her wrists to pool on the floor beneath her hands.

He swiftly bound her ankles with another cord, then pushed her over and pried the gold ring from her finger. He slid the ring onto his own little finger and held it up, admiring it with eerie intensity. "But this—" he shook his head "—*this* was a mistake. And I'm not making another."

She fought past the pain and the nausea rising in her throat. She had no doubt that he intended to kill her. He'd never leave a witness alive.

Her only defense was time.

Had Michael listened to her messages yet? Had he heard enough, over the static-filled connection?

"At least tell me—tell me what happened here," she pleaded. "*Please*. I…I just want to understand."

He smirked. "It doesn't matter now, does it?"

He strode out of the cabin, and his footsteps faded away. She knew, with absolutely no doubt, that he would be back and that she would be facing her last minutes here on earth.

She struggled to kick her feet apart, but the cord held fast. Then she twisted and pulled at the cord wound around her wrists. Slippery with her own blood, the cord gave—a few millimeters at best—but her hopes surged as she desperately fought for more slack. The cord bit into the tender flesh of her wrist. It stung, as sweat trickled into the abrasions.

Another millimeter? Closing her eyes tightly,

Janna prayed for help. Prayed that she could find a way to escape.

The pungent smell of gasoline burned her eyes as footsteps circled the outside of the cabin. Wade came back inside carrying an upended gasoline can, splashing fuel across the floor and letting the last few ounces spill onto her jeans and shirt.

He peeled off a pair of rubber gloves and stuffed them in his pockets. "Did you know that fingerprints can be lifted from the inside of gloves?"

He gave her a satisfied smile as he hooked the lone wooden chair in the room with the toe of his boot and drew it to the center of the room, then sat and folded his arms. "I found myself doing a lot of research over the years, worrying about this place. Worrying about what someone might find. Now, it'll finally be over. Your boyfriend will simply find a cabin burned to the ground and your charred remains. So sad."

"He'll figure it out." She fought to control her rising panic. "You'll get the death penalty for this."

Wade paused, pulled a handgun out of his pocket and began methodically wiping off his fingerprints with a cloth handkerchief. "Actually, no. You were distraught over your financial troubles over this place, so you decided a bullet would be an easy way out. And when you fell, you knocked over a lantern and started the fire. I'll be happy to tell everyone about how I counseled you to close the resort from the very start. Which is true, of course."

She'd managed to inch back against the wall and pull herself into a half-upright position where her hands were out of sight. She kept moving enough to mask her struggles against the cord binding her wrist. "This is crazy. You have a good career. You're respected. You said yourself that you took care of the evidence—no one would ever associate you with those bones."

He watched her struggle for a moment with an expression of disgust. "You can't get away, you know. You might as well give up."

A corner of his mouth twitched, but his eyes were flat and emotionless. "See, if you'd been smart, you would've felt threatened by everything that happened out here, and now you'd be living in town and looking forward to old age." He tipped his head in amusement. "Or if I'd been lucky, you would've simply died in that rock slide. But that's just the way things go, isn't it?"

She stared at him as he expertly dropped the clip of the gun and began snapping in its ammunition, one by one. When the clip was full, he rammed it into the butt of the gun and laid the weapon on the handkerchief in his lap and wiped the prints once again.

"This nearly got that fool kid killed, but he still doesn't know what it is." Wade pulled an old knife out of his pocket and held it up to admire its etched silver case. "But I got it back, so now I might let him live."

Horror lanced through her at the thought of Ian

and Lauren coming back to the lodge. Calling for her. Searching the cabins with rising uncertainty and worry—only to walk in on this madman and his gun.

As quickly as it had started, the rain slowed to a drizzle and the wind dropped, though daylight had now faded to dusk.

She could hear the faint sound of a motor in the distance. Michael—or his defenseless son? She kicked at a broom handle on the floor to distract Wade, but he lifted his chin and listened. Clearly, he had heard it, too.

He turned to the doorway, the gun held low at his side. In that brief moment she managed to gather her legs under her. The cord sliced deep into her wrist but now, slippery with her blood, it slid down.

A half inch.

Another.

Please, God—help me! Help me protect those kids—

Wade pivoted toward her as if he'd heard her thoughts. He crossed the room in three strides and grabbed at her shirt, took a furtive glance behind him, then pulled back a fist and rammed it into her temple.

The room spun wildly as pain exploded through her head.

Then everything went black.

He smelled smoke before he even stopped his patrol car. Michael opened the door and stepped half way out.

He scanned the resort grounds. There wasn't another car in sight, though Janna usually parked out front.

The cabins and lodge were dark. Nothing moved, though from inside the lodge he could hear the sound of Maggie's frantic barking.

There was something else in the air—the acrid scent of a fire started with gasoline as an accelerant.

Arson.

But the smell wasn't coming from the lodge. It was drifting down from somewhere up the hill. He released the safety on his Ruger and slid out of the car, quietly shutting the door.

Then he crouched low and slipped through the lowering darkness into the pine trees skirting the fence yard behind the lodge. At the far edge he glanced back and caught a metallic glint behind the house. Janna's truck—but there was another vehicle, too, parked at a crazy angle behind hers as if to prevent her escape.

Given the disjointed message she'd left on his voice mail, he knew it wasn't his imagination. Where was she—hiding in the darkened lodge? Trapped somewhere up the hill in a burning cabin?

He held perfectly still. Listened. Now the stench of burning asphalt shingles wafted from the hill, and he instinctively ran in that direction.

Past the trees, the glow of a raging fire pulsed through the heat-shattered windows of Cabin Two. Flames licked up the outside walls.

In an explosion of intense heat, a fireball burst

through the roof, shattering into fireworks of flaming embers that shot into the sky. The roof imploded, and then flames inside shot even higher. Nothing could have survived the inferno.

No one.

His heart nearly wrenched out of his chest at the sight, even as he methodically jerked his two-way radio off his belt and called for fire trucks and backup.

This kind of intense fire could only have been set.

A possible scenario unfolded in his mind in horrific detail as he imagined Janna running for her life, someone overtaking her, dragging her to the ground with animal force, then killing her—or leaving her in that cabin to die an agonizing death.

He swallowed hard, his hands on his knees.

The enormity of that possibility literally took his breath away. The aching hole in his heart took over his whole being, until he felt as if he could fall straight into the abyss.

Except, maybe she'd escaped. He had to believe it. *Please Lord, let her be all right!*

If she was alive, she was still in danger. She could be badly wounded…hiding somewhere. Bleeding to death.

Or she could be in the hands of her attacker this very minute, fighting for her life.

Off to the right he saw a flicker of movement. His heart leaped with joy as he grasped at the possibility. *Janna?*

Cold logic slid back into place with the next breath. If it wasn't her, it was likely someone with a weapon. Someone who could lead Michael to her, maybe. He whirled around and started through the underbrush, crouching low and moving parallel to the path of who—or what—he'd seen.

He froze. Listened.

Then zeroed in on the sound and kept moving, his gun drawn. The other footsteps were heavy. More careless now, as if the person sensed his presence and was starting to panic.

They were nearing the lodge—where there would be little cover. The footsteps suddenly stopped. Had the suspect reached the lawn, where his footfalls would be nearly silent?

A flash of movement appeared at the far corner of the lodge, followed by the lilt of feminine laughter and the deeper laugh of an adolescent male. *Ian and Lauren.*

"So, you're all here together—how perfect." His voice oddly calm, Wade Hollister stepped out of the trees, his gun hand pointing toward the teenagers. "Drop your weapon, Robertson, or your son will be the first to die."

EIGHTEEN

Dropping his weapon wouldn't save his son or Lauren.

Too far away to have heard Wade's threat, they stood at the corner of the lodge—perfect targets in white T-shirts that glowed under the security light, their easy laughter floating on the night breeze.

Moving silently, Michael crouched low and edged closer. Another ten yards, the right timing, and he could take the guy down.

"I guess we're at an impasse, Robertson," Wade's voice rose, tinged with hysteria. "I want you where I can see you—out there on the grass."

From his vantage point, Michael could see the man slowly panning his surroundings with his upraised gun locked in both hands. He appeared rock steady and deliberate, and Michael's estimation of the threat he posed increased a notch.

The gun swung back toward the lodge. Michael heard the click of a safety release. "Run, Ian! Run!"

Ian and Lauren startled, whirled toward Michael's voice and froze. A shot rang out, splintering the wood siding just inches from Ian's head. Lauren screamed. Jolted into action, both teenagers raced around the side of the lodge and disappeared.

"I didn't miss, Sheriff," Wade said softly. "I never do. You're the only person who can identify me at the scene, so we need to take care of that."

"It's over, Wade." Michael couldn't keep the bitterness out of his voice. "Now put down your gun, and we can talk this out."

"I don't think so." Apparently following the sound of Michael's voice, Wade turned and pulled the trigger. A bullet shattered a trunk just to Michael's left.

Michael dropped and rolled, then circled to the right, moving ever closer, his gun drawn. At a slight rustle of leaves to the left, he stilled. The sound of a familiar, muffled sneeze made him turn slightly, and he felt his heart nearly tumble to the ground. *Janna?*

She was dirty and bloodied, with a dark shadow on the side of her face that might be a massive bruise by tomorrow. But she was *alive*.

He closed his eyes for a split second in a prayer of thanks, then motioned her back. She shook her head. Pointed, then hefted a rock and threw it far to the left.

Wade spun toward the sound and Michael rushed him from behind, knocking him flat. In a heartbeat, he set Wade's weapon aside and handcuffed him, then dragged him to his feet and hauled him out onto the lawn, where weak light from the solitary security light filtered through the trees.

Rage rushed through Michael, hot and fierce, nearly overwhelming him with the temptation to plow a fist into the man's gut.

He forced his clenched fists to relax, then managed a cold smile. "Wade Hollister, you are under arrest, and I can't wait to start counting up the charges—starting with attempted murder and arson."

"Try. It's my word against yours." His eyes held a crazed gleam as he bared his teeth in a semblance of a smile. "Did my gun go off accidentally? Will you find any prints? A good lawyer has little to fear from someone like you."

Janna moved to Michael's side and looked up into his face. "I was so afraid for you," he whispered. "When I realized what was happening, I couldn't get here fast enough!"

He shook his head, scarcely able to believe the miracle standing before him, and pulled her into his arms for a gentle embrace.

She flinched, then sagged against his chest, and at the same moment he realized that her entire arm was sticky and dark with what felt like blood.

"It's okay—just a cut from a fall in that cabin. It probably doesn't even need stitches." She managed a weak smile. "Though I suppose I'd better check on my tetanus shots."

Sirens wailed discordantly in the distance, the nightmarish sound drawing closer.

He gently cupped her head in his hands. "I thought you were in the fire. I thought you were—"

"Almost." She touched a fingertip to his lips and smiled. "But the good Lord must have more things planned for me on earth, because I managed to crawl out just in time. What took so long afterward was trying to untie the cords on my wrists and ankles."

She lifted her gaze to where Wade stood, his chin lifted defiantly and his eyes cold. "You won't have any trouble getting testimony at his trial, because I'll be there with bells on. Quick," she added in a whisper. "See if he still has a gold ring on his little finger."

Michael immediately turned toward Wade and closed the distance between them, then stepped behind him and examined the man's hands.

"Looking for something?" Wade's laugh held a note of derision. "Like I said, you'll have trouble proving anything."

The ring was gone.

A night in the slammer had an interesting effect on Wade Hollister. Initially cocky, belligerent and threatening all manner of lawsuits, blustering that he would certainly be defending himself, his arraignment in the morning appeared to bring reality into greater focus. Maybe the ring would have been useful evidence, but Janna's testimony and the other evidence was clearly sufficient.

The one-million-dollar bail, based on charges of double murder, attempted murder and arson, proved to be an even stronger wake-up call.

By morning, he was pacing his cell—turning noticeably gray when Michael told him the ring had been found. By midafternoon he was asking to contact a criminal defense lawyer and was ready to talk.

Michael mulled over the events of the past couple of days as he waited for Janna to come out of the doctor's office. He felt edgy until she appeared in the waiting room, then had to hold back the need to sweep her into an embrace and never let her go. "Is Tessa coming back, or do you need a ride home?"

"She took the kids over to the store for a few minutes, but thanks anyway," Janna said, awkwardly reaching around to drape her sweater over her shoulders. "Good news—the doctor says my wound is healing well. No signs of infection, and the stitches can come out in a few days."

Michael took the sweater from her and shook it, then settled it gently into place. "It could've all been so much worse. I can't stop thinking about what happened—what could've happened. It's just a miracle that you came out of the cabin alive."

"I didn't stop praying for a minute, once I came to. The roof collapsed just seconds after I got out." She smiled up at him. "Any more news?"

He offered her the crook of his arm, and they strolled out of the doctor's office into the late June sunshine. But instead of ushering her to his truck, Michael steered her over to the privacy of a park bench surrounded by tiger lilies before saying anything more.

"When Wade knew he was going to be caught, he threw the ring out into the trees. My deputies found it using a metal detector. Once we had it, we were able to find its owner, and now Wade's singing like the proverbial canary."

"Is she—" Janna's voice caught.

"We found her remains this afternoon, buried close to Cabin Ten."

Tears shimmered in her eyes. "I was hoping you'd find her happily living out East."

"Unfortunately, no…which is why Wade was so worried about the lodge opening. When you asked him about septic system regulations, he probably feared that backhoe work might uncover her grave. So then he escalated."

"The rock slide?"

"To scare you into leaving the lodge, or simply eliminate you altogether."

Janna shivered. "He almost succeeded."

"I just wish I'd gotten my answers sooner. This afternoon I learned that he was the one buying those imported cigarettes. Then I got your message and went to his office, but he was already gone."

"He tailed me back to the lodge," Janna said with a shudder. "So he's the one who sabotaged the backhoe?"

"Fingerprints will probably prove it. He was no doubt the cause of most of your problems, Janna... though he denies ever breaking into Cabin Ten before you moved here. The trashy magazines and liquor bottles were probably left by some vagrant—or maybe, kids who came out to party. The faded stains on the floor were red wine, not blood."

Janna pulled her sweater tighter around her shoulders. "Do you know anything about the owner of the ring?"

"She was a college girl, out West on a spring-break road trip. Her girlfriend got sick and caught a plane home, so she had to drive back alone."

"How on earth did she end up out here?"

"Conjecture so far, but at the time, Snow Canyon Lodge was closed, and even back then, apparently, there were some wild parties out there, far away from the eyes of the law. Maybe that's why some of the locals haven't been forthcoming about the past. No longer able to recall exact details, they might be afraid they'd incriminate relatives or old friends."

"But Wade..." Janna shook her head. "I still don't get it. I've always thought he was a nice guy."

"Wade either invited her or met her there, and somehow lured her out to the farthest cabin for some private action. He claims she wanted to play, but from all accounts she was a girl who never would've done anything like that. He says she 'went crazy,' and things got out of hand." He hesitated. "It…was fairly clear from the remains that he'd beaten her badly. Some broken bones, and it looked to me like a fractured skull."

Janna rested her fingertips at her mouth, her eyes stricken. "That's so awful."

"He buried the body in a panic, but was too drunk and scared to remember exactly where. All this time, he's been afraid that he left evidence behind. Sure enough, he did."

"What about the other remains?"

"A backpacker rambling throughout the West. He saw Wade disposing of the body, so Wade stabbed him, then buried that body, too, but during the fight he lost his grandfather's monogrammed knife."

"Wade said something about finding it in your cabin." Janna wrapped her arms around her waist and looked up at Michael, her voice filled with sadness. "What if he'd hurt Ian?"

"That could've happened, because Wade's guilt and fear have been growing for years. He panicked when he heard the lodge was reopening, and started searching with a metal detector. Found all sorts of little metal things, though not what he was after."

"Then how did Ian get it?"

"The detector had just started clicking again when Ian showed up. Wade ran to avoid being recognized.

Ian discovered the knife and kept it for over a month. He never told me."

"I feel like such a fool. Wade acted like he was concerned about our welfare, but all along he was lying. If I'd been smarter, none of us would've been in danger." She drew in a shaky breath. "And what about the people in town, all those years ago? Did no one at that party notice him with an unfamiliar girl? See that he went home alone or think he acted strangely?"

"I've talked to a lot of people who lived here at the time. When I asked about Wade, they all got a little edgy. His dad was once very influential in these parts and wielded a lot of power. So even if anyone suspected something back then, they probably wouldn't have dared testify against the man's son."

"I want to believe in people," she said in a broken voice. "But after this, I'll always wonder."

They both fell silent.

There were a hundred things he wanted to say to her, but he didn't even know where to begin.

"I know it's been hard, dealing with your job and my problems at Snow Canyon," Janna said, turning to him. "But we'll be fine now, if you want to move into town. You can rip up that silly penalty clause for the early departure fee." A sad smile tipped up a corner of her mouth. "I hope we can still be friends, though."

"I don't want that, Janna." At the flash of surprise and hurt in her eyes, he winced at his poor choice of words. "I couldn't sleep last night, because all I could think about was the fact that I'd nearly lost you forever. And if I don't make things right, it could still happen."

The flicker of hope in her expression gave him the courage to continue. "During the last year I've struggled a lot with my faith. I haven't been able to forgive myself for Ian's disabilities and Elise's death, because it's my fault Ian was behind the wheel. That guilt has been with me every minute of every day. I just couldn't understand why God let all of that happen."

"Oh, Michael. Most parents buy their teenagers a car…and bad things don't happen to all of them. He was just in the wrong place at the wrong time."

"I think you said something like that to me a while ago, but I wasn't ready to listen, because I'd failed my family so badly." He exhaled slowly. "I was still overwhelmed with grief, and I couldn't see how that would ever change. How could it? The accident could never be reversed. Nothing could bring Elise back or make Ian whole again. God could not give me what I wanted most."

Resting a hand against his cheek, Janna searched his face, her eyes filled with compassion…and something much deeper that seemed to reach out and touch his heart. "And now?"

"Thinking you'd died in that fire and seeing Wade shoot at Ian shook me right to the core. But God answered my prayers, just as He always has. I've just been too blind and stubborn to always see His answers." Beneath her loving touch, he felt the healing balm of forgiveness and grace spread through him, warming him. Making him feel complete. "His forgiveness has always been right in front of me, too. I've just been too busy blaming myself to accept it."

She nodded. "Last night I realized a few things, too. The whole time, I was praying for rescue and for the child I might never see again. God's answer was giving me a way to escape and the strength to do it on my own. I still can't believe I made it out that window in time."

"For which I will be forever grateful." Michael stood and offered her his hand. When she rose, he curved his arms around her in a gentle embrace, and tucked her head beneath his chin. It felt so perfect, so right to hold her, that his heart seemed to swell until it filled his chest.

She pulled back and gave him a rueful smile. "Since last night, one thought has been running through my head. Why do I ever doubt Him? There was never any love in my childhood home, and ever since my husband left, I've been afraid of risking another failure. But that isn't the way God wants His children to live—and I could have missed a chance with you if all of this hadn't happened."

Her words filled him with happiness and promised a chance at a future he'd never thought possible. "I love you, Janna. I don't think I realized it until I nearly lost you."

She leaned forward to brush a kiss against Michael's cheek. "And I love you, too—more than words could ever say."

Something stirred behind them, and they both turned as one to see Tessa standing on the sidewalk with Ian and Rylie.

They were all grinning.

"Wow," Rylie breathed. "Does that mean I'll have a *brother?*"

Ian tugged on her ponytail, his grin widening into a broad smile. "Lucky you, kid."

"It does, if Janna agrees." Michael held his breath, felt his own eyes burn when he saw the answer in hers—the promise of a lifetime of love waiting to be explored.

She grinned. "Yes!"

A feeling of thankfulness and completion swept through him, so powerful and overwhelming that it felt as if the Lord's glory was shining down on all of them, blessing them with a future filled with joy.

Michael opened his arms and welcomed Janna and the children into an embrace—and felt as if he'd truly come home at last.

* * * * *

Come back to the Snow Canyon Ranch
in February 2008!
Leigh McAllister comes home in VENDETTA.

Dear Reader,

Welcome to Wolf Creek, Wyoming! Though the town is fictitious, it's set near the Tetons, which are part of the Rocky Mountains. This area is so incredibly beautiful, so stunning, that it takes my breath away every time I visit. The Lord's magnificence is everywhere—in the rugged peaks, the clear, still lakes, the sweeping vistas and sparkling mountain streams.

I love writing mystery and suspense, with a backdrop of intergenerational family relationships. *Hard Evidence* is the first of three books involving sisters who grew up as the daughters of a tough, no-nonsense, widowed ranchwoman. Claire McAllister had to be strong and focused to keep her ranch going, but at what sacrifice to her children?

Estranged for many years, her daughters are now coming together to care for her, but the phrase "you can't really go home again" certainly applies in the darkest sense to these young women. Each must face unexpected dangers. Each must embark on a journey of faith to finally reach the life of love and abundant living that God wishes for us all.

None of us can change the past, take back the words we've said or the hurtful things we've done. But the power of love, faith and prayer is truly beyond all understanding!

Wishing you blessings and peace,

Roxanne

QUESTIONS FOR DISCUSSION

1. Janna and her two sisters had a difficult childhood, growing up in a single-parent household, with a mother who wasn't warm and nurturing. They are now trying to strengthen their family bonds. Have you ever been separated from members of your family due to interpersonal conflicts? Were you able to resolve those issues?

2. Claire McAllister faced the loss of two husbands and a life of hardship, while running a ranch on her own and raising three daughters. She had great determination and a strong work ethic and provided well for her family. Still, she grew away from her faith over the years, ended up with few friends and has long been estranged from two of her daughters. What are your thoughts on Claire and her worldly success? Do you know of anyone in your family or your community who has made similar choices? How did it affect their marriage and their children?

3. Claire is now slipping into dementia, and the doctor suspects the start of Alzheimer's. Do you have relatives or friends with a similar diagnosis? How does this affect the family?

4. Wade has carried a burden of guilt for many years, and in this story he faces escalating fear over the possible discovery of the truth. In a sense, these emotions have created a darker prison for him than the physical one he has desperately tried to avoid. Have you ever done something that you regretted? How did you handle that situation? Can we always go to God in prayer and receive His forgiveness?

5. Janna often prays for guidance and help. How often do you pray? And how has God answered?

6. Despite the efforts of Janna and the sheriff's department, the final key to the mystery is the discovery of an old ring—a tiny object that easily could have been overlooked and lost forever, or simply dismissed by Janna and her daughter. Was the discovery an answer to Janna's prayers, or just chance?

7. Michael feels a deep sense of guilt over his son's car accident. He'd wanted to give his son a gift, but it ended in tragedy. Have you ever made decisions that have ended badly for someone you love?

8. Claire turned away from God long ago, and is a prideful, embittered and lonely woman. She ut-

ters a prayer just once in this story—when she is faced with the fear of her increasing dementia. How could her life be different now, if she turns back to God and develops a stronger relationship with Him? Is it ever too late? Does it take a crisis for some people to open their hearts to faith?

9. Think back over your own life. Did tragedy and hardship every bring about good things in your life? Did it bring you closer to God?

10. Ian had been scarred emotionally and physically by his car accident and feels tremendous guilt over the death of his mother. If you could sit with him for just an hour, what could you say to him about God's love, acceptance and forgiveness that would ease his burdens?

There was something about the young woman—something he couldn't put his finger on. He'd hardly glanced at her when he'd hauled her from the family sleigh, but now he took a longer look through the veil of falling snow.

For a moment her silhouette, her size, and her movements all reminded him of Noelle. How about that. Noelle, his frozen heart reminded him with a painful squeeze, had been his first—and only—love.

It couldn't be her, he reasoned, since she was married and probably a mother by now. She'd be safe in town, living snug in one of the finest houses in the county instead of riding along the country roads in a storm. Still, curiosity nibbled at him, and he plowed through the knee-deep snow. Snow was falling faster now, and yet somehow through the thick downfall his gaze seemed to find her.

She was fragile, a delicate bundle of wool—and snow clung to her hood and scarf and cloak like a shroud, making her tough to see. She'd been just a little bit of a thing when he'd lifted her from the sleigh and his only thought at the time had been to get both women out of danger. Now something chewed at his memory. He couldn't quite figure out what, but he could feel it in his gut.

The woman was talking on as she unwound her niece's veil. "We were tossed about dreadfully. You're likely bruised and broken from root to stem. I've never been so terrified. All I could do was pray over and over and think of you, my dear." Her words warmed with tenderness. "What a greater nightmare for you."

"We're fine. All's well that ends well," the niece insisted.

Although her voice was muffled by the thick snowfall, his step faltered. There was something about her voice, something familiar in the gentle resonance of her alto. Now he could see the top part of her face, due to her loosened scarf. Her eyes—they were startling, flawless emerald green.

Whoa, there. He'd seen that perfect shade of green before—and long ago. Recognition speared through his midsection, but he already knew she was Noelle even before the last layer of the scarf fell away from her face.

His Noelle, just as lovely and dear, was now blind and veiled with snow. His first love. The woman he'd spent years and thousands of miles trying to forget. Hard to believe that there she was suddenly right in front of him. He'd heard about the engagement announcement a few years back, and he'd known in returning to live in Angel Falls that he'd have to run into her eventually.

He just didn't figure it would be so soon and like this.

Seeing her again shouldn't make him feel as if he'd been hit in the chest with a cannonball. The shock was wearing off, he realized, the same as when you received a hard blow. First off, you were too stunned to feel it. Then the pain began to settle in, just a hint, and then rushing until it was unbearable. Yep, that was the word to describe what was happening inside his rib cage. A pain worse than a broken bone beat through him.

Best get the sleigh righted, the horse hitched back up and the women home. But it was all he could do to turn his back as he took his mustang by the bridle. The palomino pinto gave him a snort and shook his head, sending the snow on his golden mane flying.

Yep, I know how you feel, Sunny, Thad thought. Judging by the look of things, it would be a long time until they had a chance to get out of the cold.

He'd do his best to ignore the women, especially Noelle, and to get to the work needin' to be done. He gave the sleigh a shove, but the vehicle was wedged against the snow-covered brush banking the river. Not that he'd put a lot of weight on the Lord over much these days, but Thad had to admit it was a close call. Almost eerie how he'd caught them just in time. It did seem providential. Had they gone only a few feet more, gravity would have done the trick and pulled the sleigh straight into the frigid, fast waters of Angel River and plummeted them directly over the tallest falls in the territory.

Thad squeezed his eyes shut. He couldn't stand to think of Noelle tossed into that river, fighting the powerful current along with the ice chunks. There would have been no way to have pulled her from the river in time. Had he been a few minutes slower in coming after them or if Sunny hadn't been so swift, there would have been no way to save her. To fate, to the Lord or to simple chance, he was grateful.

Some tiny measure of tenderness in his chest, like a fire long banked, sputtered to life. His tenderness for her was still there, after so much time and distance. How about that.

Since the black gelding was a tad calmer now that the sound of the train had faded off into the distance, Thad rehitched him to the sleigh but secured the driving reins to his saddle horn. He used the two horses working together to free the sleigh and get it realigned toward the road.

The older woman looked uncertain about getting back into the vehicle. With the way that black gelding of theirs was twitchy and wild-eyed, he didn't blame her. "Don't worry, ma'am, I'll see you two ladies home."

"Th-that would be very good of you, sir. I'm rather shaken up. I've half a mind to walk the entire mile home, except for my dear niece."

Noelle. He wouldn't let his heart react to her. All that mattered was doing right by her—and that was one thing that hadn't changed. He came around to help the aunt into the sleigh, and after she was safely seated, turned toward Noelle. Her scarf slid down to reveal the curve of her face, the slope of her nose and the rosebud smile of her mouth.

What had happened to her? How had she lost her sight? Sadness filled him for her blindness and for what could have been between them once. He thought about saying something to her, so she would know who he was, but what good would that do? The past was done and over. Only the emptiness of it remained.

"Thank you so much, sir." She turned toward the sound of his step and smiled in his direction. If she, too, wondered who he was, she gave no real hint of it.

He didn't expect her to. Chances were she hardly remembered him, and if she did, she wouldn't think too well of him. She would never know what good wishes he wanted for her as he took her gloved hand. The layers of wool and leather and sheepskin lining between his hand and hers didn't stop that tiny flame of tenderness for her in his chest from growing a notch.

He looked into her eyes, into Noelle's eyes, the woman he'd loved truly so long ago, knowing she did not recognize him. Could not see him or sense him, even at heart. She smiled at him as if he were the Good Samaritan she thought he was as he helped her settle onto the seat.

Love was an odd thing, he realized as he backed away. Once their love had been an emotion felt so strong and pure and true that he would have vowed on his very soul that nothing could tarnish nor diminish their bond. But time had done that simply, easily, and they stood now as strangers.

* * * * *

*Don't miss this deeply moving
Love Inspired Historical story about
a young woman in 1883 Montana who reunites
with an old beau and soon discovers that love
is the greatest blessing of all.*

*HOMESPUN BRIDE
By Jillian Hart
Available February 2008*

*And also look for
THE BRITON
by Catherine Palmer,
about a medieval lady who battles for
her family legacy—and finds true love.*

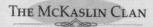

REQUEST YOUR FREE BOOKS!
2 FREE RIVETING INSPIRATIONAL NOVELS PLUS 2 FREE MYSTERY GIFTS

Love Inspired®
SUSPENSE

YES! Please send me 2 FREE Love Inspired® Suspense novels and my 2 FREE mystery gifts. After receiving them, if I don't wish to receive any more books, I can return the shipping statement marked "cancel." If I don't cancel, I will receive 4 brand-new novels every month and be billed just $3.99 per book in the U.S. or $4.74 per book in Canada, plus 25¢ shipping and handling per book and applicable taxes, if any*. That's a savings of 20% off the cover price! I understand that accepting the 2 free books and gifts places me under no obligation to buy anything. I can always return a shipment and cancel at any time. Even if I never buy another book from Steeple Hill, the two free books and gifts are mine to keep forever.

123 IDN EL5H 323 IDN ELQH

Name _____ (PLEASE PRINT)

Address _____ Apt. #

City _____ State/Prov. _____ Zip/Postal Code

Signature (if under 18, a parent or guardian must sign)

Order online at www.LoveInspiredSuspense.com

Or mail to Steeple Hill Reader Service™:

IN U.S.A.: P.O. Box 1867, Buffalo, NY 14240-1867
IN CANADA: P.O. Box 609, Fort Erie, Ontario L2A 5X3

Not valid to current Love Inspired Suspense subscribers.

**Want to try two free books from another series?
Call 1-800-873-8635 or visit www.morefreebooks.com**

* Terms and prices subject to change without notice. NY residents add applicable sales tax. Canadian residents will be charged applicable provincial taxes and GST. This offer is limited to one order per household. All orders subject to approval. Credit or debit balances in a customer's account(s) may be offset by any other outstanding balance owed by or to the customer. Please allow 4 to 6 weeks for delivery.

Your Privacy: Steeple Hill is committed to protecting your privacy. Our Privacy Policy is available online at www.eHarlequin.com or upon request from the Reader Service. From time to time we make our lists of customers available to reputable firms who may have a product or service of interest to you. If you would prefer we not share your name and address, please check here. ☐

LISUS07

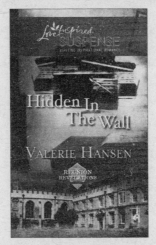

Love Inspired

TITLES AVAILABLE NEXT MONTH

Don't miss these four stories in January

FAMILY IN HIS HEART by Gail Gaymer Martin
Nick Thornton could tell Rona Meyers was a special person, so
he'd offered her a much-needed job. And as he got to know her, he
couldn't stop wondering if God was offering him a new beginning
and a second chance at love.

NEXT DOOR DADDY by Debra Clopton
A Mule Hollow novel
When rancher Nate Talbert prayed for a change to his reclusive
life, he got new next-door neighbor Pollyanna McDonald. But the
menagerie of pets that she and her son cared for was driving him
crazy. Could he handle the chaos that surrounded her?

THE DOCTOR'S BRIDE by Patt Marr
Everyone in town was trying to find Dr. Zack Hemingway a wife.
Yet the one girl who caught his eye wasn't interested. Why was
Chloe Kilgannon hiding from him? This doctor knew it would
take some good medicine to get to the heart of the matter.

A SOLDIER'S PROMISE by Cheryl Wyatt
Wings of Refuge
Pararescue jumper Joel Montgomery had the power to make a
sick little boy's dream come true. He was determined to follow
through even if it meant returning to a place he'd rather forget.
And meeting the boy's pretty teacher made his leap of faith
doubly worth the price.

LICNM1207